PARIS 19.

Henry Miller

June Miller, 1928 (from Henry Miller's *Paris Notebooks*)

PARIS 1928
NEXUS II

Henry Miller

Drawings by Garry Shead
Introduction by Tom Thompson

INDIANA UNIVERSITY PRESS
Bloomington and Indianapolis

HENRY MILLER

For Tony and Valentine

Published by John Libbey Publishing Ltd, United Kingdom
e-mail: john.libbey@orange.fr; web site: www.johnlibbey.com

Co-published for North America and Asia by Indiana University Press,
601 North Morton St., Bloomington, IN 47404, USA
www.iupress.indiana.edu 1-800-842-6796

Cataloging information is available from the Library of Congress

ISBN: 9780253008312

Printed and bound in China by 1010 Printing International Ltd.

Introduction

*I*n 1927, a would-be writer, Henry Miller, opened a speakeasy in Greenwich Village with his second wife June Mansfield. That year, he exhibited his first watercolours and, according to Miller, compiled notes for an entire cycle of autobiographical novels in one day. These *Capricorn Notes* became a resource and a wellspring which the writer drew on for the rest of his creative life. They became immediately useful in his second period in Paris, (1930–1939), when he published *Tropic of Cancer* (1934), *Black Spring* (1936) and *Tropic of Capricorn* (1939) and after that, with the publication of the *Rosy Crucifixion* trilogy of *Sexus* (1949), *Plexus* (1952), and *Nexus* (1960). This last was completed in April 1959 and published in France as *Nexus I* the following year. Miller's imaginative commitment to the events recorded in the *Notes* lasted for most his life, with the writer revisiting the sequence and its unfolding again and again.

Nearly thirty years after its original publication, Grove Press published the first authorized US edition of *Tropic of Cancer* in 1961. That same year, Henry Miller, now a writer of international stature, was touring Europe and working on a new book, *Nexus II*. He completed three drafts.[1] The release of *Tropic of Cancer* was keeping his publishers busy at the time, defending the author in obscenity trials in different states.

The new manuscript, *Nexus II*, was a reworking of Miller's first trip to Paris with June in 1928, a journey that had taken them deep into the Europe she saw as her homeland. Miller had already travelled over this territory in several works, notably in *Tropic of Capricorn*, where he saw their journey as a metaphor for the sinuous, multi-faceted nature of his relationship with June. *"When I look up from my machine, my eyes confront the large, many-coloured map of Europe which I have pinned to my wall; it is criss-crossed with rail and steam ship lines, with national frontiers, with indelible prejudices and rivalries. And the very raggedness of its contour ... all this strain and erosion exemplifies, in my imagination, the conflict that has been going on between Hildred (June) and myself and of which this book is but a map.*[2]

With *Tropic of Cancer, Black Spring* and *Tropic of Capricorn* using some of the material in their own incarnations, why we may ask should he have felt the need to revisit it again? What had been left unsaid?

One answer to these questions lies in the unpublished version of *Tropic of Capricorn*, where Miller stated his commitment to a discursive, digressive style, the *"vital part of me"* made up by books and writers. *"They too are in my blood"*, he wrote, *"carried along with my living, part of my hate and love"*.[3] Here, he also described *"elements creeping in which I am sure no editor would approve of. It is impossible for me to write even the most fantastic tale without mention of books and authors, without extraneous details, as it is called."*

Miller was seventy years old in 1961, his memory reignited by this new exploration of Europe. Plainly, he felt it necessary to go over the map again for any new and *"extraneous"* details that might affect his understanding of himself as a writer; a status still under attack via the obscenity trials. *Nexus II* is also a travelogue of sorts, allowing him the chance to include extraneous descriptions and reflections that are not germane to the earlier books. To that extent, it is a re-examination, both of his precarious period as a would-be writer in Paris before the Crash of 1929 and his impressions of the Europe he found on his first visit, memories sharpened by his present situation.

"I'm a writer ... a writer of no importance. I haven't yet sold a story or an article to any editor. We live by our wits ... do you know what that means? We've been hungry for days on end, we've robbed our friends, we've cheated the tradespeople, we've lived a dog's life ever since I decided to be a writer." [4]

The years preceding this declaration/confession were critical years for Miller. He had fallen in love with June Mansfield in 1923, divorcing his first wife, Beatrice Wickens, in 1924 and leaving behind his 5-year-old daughter Barbara. He married June the same year, leaving work and responsibility behind with the intention of living as a writer. Their partnership was essential to Miller, not just at the personal and creative level but because it was only through June's machinations that he was able to sell his work at all.

Nexus II opens in the summer of 1928 with Val and Mona (Henry and June) arriving in Paris on money provided by 'Pop', one of June's many admirers. 'Pop' believed June was the author of Miller's novel *Moloch*, which had been written in installments and passed off to 'Pop' as hers. The couple spent more than a year in Europe on this visit, travelling to England, France, Belgium, Germany, Czechoslovakia, Austria, Hungary and Poland.

June's persona was self created. Her birth name was Smerdt, a Russian word for death, but her preferred name was June Mansfield, which she said was from *"man's field"* or *"cemetery"*. As Miller's confidant, the photographer Brassai noted, she'd worked as *"a B-girl at a gay nightclub for both sexes in Greenwich Village, and was courted by some of the butchest lesbians around"*. Brassai recalled that June herself preferred *"seraphic-looking women and, one evening fell madly in love with a young Russian woman whom Miller would call "Anastasia" ... Henry wondered if they were planning to run away, for he knew they dreamed of Paris and of Montparnasse".*[5]

Miller described himself at the moment of his departure for Paris as *"An expatriate from Brooklyn, a francophile, a vagabond, a writer at the beginning of his career, naive, enthusiastic, absorbent as a sponge, interested in everything and seemingly rudderless".*[6] This trip was to be his first foray into the dreams and yearnings he'd conjured in their life on the fringes of New York society in the 1920s. It was underpinned by the tantalizing uncertainty of his relationship with June, whose feints, ploys and subterfuges will be familiar to all readers of Miller. Foremost of these, in this period, concerned her relationship with *"Anastasia"* or *"Stasia"*, the character based on her lover, Jean Kronski. Jean had moved in with the couple in 1927 and her surprise departure for Europe with June some months later had left Miller enraged, bereaved and helpless. This abandonment prompted him that July to draft a grand sketch of his life and his obsession with June, now known as the *Capricorn Notes*.

In due course, June cabled for Miller to join her but on this first trip he was heavily dependent on her, stumbling with the language, not knowing the territory, and captive of her dream of finding her own European background. *"If I could only see the house in which she was born"*, he wrote, *"it seemed to me it would wipe out all the lies she had ever told me".*[7]

Their journey was interlinked with other expatriate Americans whom they encountered at the same bars and the same haunts, with Miller always doubting the accidental nature of these meetings. They longed to try the pleasures of *Le Dôme*, *Les Deux Magots* or *Le Rat Mort*, only to find them crowded with Americans; many responding to a best-selling 1927 travel guide *Paris with the Lid Lifted*, which June, at least, had read.

"The Notorious Café Du Dôme ... *You see all the Nuts and all the Freaks, plain and fancy; broke and affluent, mangy and modish, glassy-eyed and goo-goo eyed; Van Dyke* [sic] *bearded and pasty-faced; decorous and degenerate; pious and perverted; mademoiselle-ish young men and young-men-ish mademoiselles ... Those who get themselves up the most grotesquely, are, 9 times out of 10, Americans."* [8]

Miller railed at these reminders of home, writing that: *"Paris was getting on my nerves more and more. Perhaps not Paris itself but the people we seemed obliged to associate with. We were always running into the same types one meets in Greenwich Village."* The couple travelled more extensively but the drama of post-war Europe infested his consciousness. *"That night I didn't sleep a wink. It wasn't the bedbugs that kept me awake, it was Europe, the horror and misery, which penetrated it through and through."* [9]

Notwithstanding this, the experience of Europe and in particular, the music of the alien, the 'Gypsy' and the 'Jew' awakened him to his task as a writer. *"If I could write like those guys fiddle I'd be the happiest man alive ... First I've got to find out who I am, where I came from, where I'm going, why I'm here. I've got to make myself an orphan, teach myself my own language, stop taking music lessons and all that. First I've got to get rid of all the baggage I've accumulated ... I mean literature. That Gypsy taught me more in a few minutes than all the volumes of Henry James, Dostoyevsky, Knut Hamsun and Peter Schlemihl combined."* [10]

For Miller, the membrane of this cosmological world could also take him back to the alternate realm of his life in New York, the Greenwich Village speakeasy and the dance mania of his recent past: *"One had to*

*be screwy to patronize such a dive. A purgatorial hole through and
through: a hole in the flap pocket of a demon whose punishment it
was to masturbate himself to death ... At home, and dancers themselves ... sashay into Central Park."* [11]

DH Lawrence's *Lady Chatterley's Lover* was published at the same
time as Miller's first visit to Europe and while he disputed Lawrence's
mystification of sex, he was entranced by the power of the writing,
especially the opening passage which he would echo in the opening to
Tropic of Cancer:

*"Ours is essentially a tragic age, so we refuse to take it tragically. The
cataclysm has happened, we are among the ruins, we start to build up
new little habitats, to have new little hopes. It is rather hard work,
there is now no smooth road into the future; but we go around, or
scramble over the obstacles. We've got to live, no matter how many
skies have fallen."* [12]

Miller made an intense study of Lawrence[13] during his second period
in Paris, completing it before June left him and filed for divorce in
1933. The spectre of obscenity hung over *Lady Chatterley's Lover*
until 1960, a fact that would have resonated with Miller when Grove
chose to excise twenty-three manuscript pages from the authorized
US edition of the original *Nexus "due to its sexual content"*.[14] One
of the incidents described occurs after June had left for Europe with
Jean, and Miller is on his own, prowling New York's streets and parks.

*"In the midst of these reflections I remember the Park again, two girls
sitting on a knoll just above me"*, he wrote. *"One has her legs bent like
a jack-knife, she's fully exposed. Reclining on an elbow, I pretend to
be studying a blade of grass ... More and more the whole thing seemed
like a dream. A delicious wet dream. I could well imagine what lay in
store for me. But why me? What had I done to deserve this?*

The meeting progresses to a *bacchanal* in the women's apartment where the writer has cause for reflection.

"For an instant Mona flitted through my mind. If she could see me now! And she, what was she doing at this moment? Further specula-tion on that score was interrupted by Suzanne's entrance. She had rigged herself up in a fetching negligee. As she fixed herself a drink she looked at me, as if approvingly and said: 'You're married, aren't you?'"

"Amy smiled indulgently. 'Suzanne is truly lecherous', she said, licking her words. "I don't think any man can satisfy her. When she's really hot, why ... well, I've seen her take a ..." She turned and pointed to a long, thin black candle standing on the chest of drawers."

Any repeat of this adventure is stopped in its tracks by a cablegram from June arriving back from Paris – *"Meet Me"*.

Apart from the 'obscene' content of their work, Miller shared with Lawrence a life-transforming partnership with a woman that led him towards a literature of personal redemption. Reviled in their own countries, both writers insisted on freedom of expression; the freedom to talk openly and frankly according to their vision. This freedom was being tested in the courts throughout Miller's early and mid career as a writer.

Nexus II charts the first journey again, following the travelers until, after a year of high living, June gives their last $20 to a gypsy violinist, leaving them flat broke and living on the kindness of a Negro shoeshine. The American Consulate won't assist them and once again it's 'Pop' who sends the funds that allow them to return to Paris for the summer of 1929. They find it crawling with Americans bent on a similar quest.

Fleeing they travel down the Rhine to Vienna and on towards Hungary where the poor and dispossessed still struggle with 'their' Europe. There the farce of his situation descends; an unpublished writer, dependent on his wife's admirers as she peddles his words as hers. In Romania and later staying with relatives of June, their plight grinds his imagination to a halt. Miller ponders what they are *"doing here in this God-awful hole. ... I would wonder, and remember ... just how we had got here ..."*.

This locks the circuit back to those moments alone in New York's Central Park and the women who entice him back to their lair. *Nexus II* ends in the Balkans, with Miller and June counting down the months to the Great Crash of October 1929, which will catapult them back to the United States.

Nexus II will be a delight for any Miller fan, opening up fresh vantage points on the earlier works. For new readers, in a less-repressive century, the novel will provide an introduction to one of the most picaresque writers of modern English.

Tom Thompson
Sydney, April 2012

Notes

1 *Nexus II*, noted as A23 in *Henry Miller: A Personal Archive* (Roger Jackson & William Ashley) *(HM:APA)*; the variants being pages 1–87, a second draft carbon pages 1–112, and a typed fragment pages 87–115.

2 Noted as A4 in *HM:APA*.

3 Unpublished draft of *Tropic of Capricorn*, 1934, noted as A4 in *HM:APA*.

4 *Paris 1928*, page 77.

5 *Henry Miller: The Paris Years* by Brassaï (Arcade, 1995).

6 *Big Sur and the Oranges of Hieronymus Bosch* by Henry Miller (New Directions, 1957) page 277.

7 *Paris 1928*, page 128.

8 Bruce Reynolds: *Paris with the Lid Lifted* (George Sully, NY 1927), page 204.

9 *Paris 1928*, page 108.

10 *Paris 1928*, page 121.

11 *Paris 1928*, page 131.

12 *Lady Chatterley's Lover*, Florence 1928, page 1.

13 Henry Miller: *Notes on Aaron's Rod* (Black Sparrow, 1980) and *The World of Lawrence* (Capra Press, 1980).

14 *HM:APA*, noted as A22, being pages 258–281 from Miller's original manuscript for *Nexus I*, and placed here in Miller's preferred sequence.

Henry Miller, 1936

HENRY MILLER

Part One:
Vacation Abroad

S o this is it, I said I to myself, coming down the gangplank at Le Havre ready to set foot on French soil. *Europe!* Though I had been preparing for it for seven days, and before that for seventy-seven years or centuries, I could scarcely believe my eyes. No child could welcome its mother with more eagerness than I welcomed the sight of Europe. At last my dream had come true. I was there, and with money in my wallet. And she was with me, Mona, perhaps not as excited as I, but radiant and looking as bizarre as ever in her flowing black cape, her eyes heavily made up, her barbaric jewellery swinging from neck and wrists.

It wasn't a pretty sight, the dock yards, with lumber and merchandise piled up in every direction, but it was different. And that was what I craved — something different. As we stumbled over the tracks to get to the boat train I caught sight of the purser, garbed now in civilian clothes, satchel in hand, picking his way to God knows where, perhaps the nearest bistrot. He looked like a different person now — Mister Anybody — as he mooched along. On the boat he had been somebody, witty, entertaining, a man to answer any and every question — and an excellent chess player too. Now he was just one more Frenchman, a very ordinary Frenchman, with a peak cap and trousers that were too short. Above his head floated the gray-black roofs which were to become so dear to me in time. Not a pretty picture, but solid, comfy, everything built to last, it seemed. On the whole somewhat shabby, tawdry, woe-begone. But that was part of the image of Europe which I had always preserved.

Rolling toward Paris my eyes were glued to the window pane. The countryside seemed neat and orderly, the little railway stations were just as one finds them in picture books, the cows and sheep were like cows and sheep anywhere, but the humans appeared always to be draped in mourning. Now and then, usually from factory windows, the French blue sang out, a blue such as I had never seen before. Now and then the tricolor popped up, usually atop some ugly building. A beautiful flag – light, airy, joyous, and so simple in design.

Nearing Paris Mona gave me a nudge and pointed to a cluster of shimmering white buildings which overlooked the city. The Sacré Coeur. At once my heart leaped; tears came to my eyes. I don't know why I felt such emotion – there was nothing about Sacré Coeur which had any claim on me. Perhaps it was simply the fact that it belonged to Montmartre. That was indeed a magic word for me. Montmartre.

Instantly I thought of George Moore, Van Gogh, Utrillo, of all the painters, poets, vagabonds I had ever read about. "Are we going to live there?" I asked. She didn't think so. It was too far from the center of things. Well, I would walk there every day, I fervidly thought to myself. And where was the center, I wondered. Surely we weren't going to live near the Opera and the American Express?

St. Lazare. We had arrived. I gasped as I took a quick look around. It was the rush hour and the place was jumping. I kept looking up all the time. The glass roof fascinated me. Never had I seen a railway station like this. Standing at the curb, waiting for the porter to get us a cab. I could have stayed in that spot forever. All Paris seemed to be parading before my eyes. This was it.

Suddenly I felt completely lost. It was no longer Europe, France, Paris, but a maelstrom in which I was drowning, without knowing so much as how to say 'Help! Help!' (It took me months, indeed. to discover that the word for 'Help!' is '*Au secours!*' What I thought of was 'Alp! Alp!' which is nightmare in some strange language. (Wasn't it Strindberg shivering in the wintry boughs of a tree who kept yelling 'Alp! Alp!')

We are threading our way through the maze of traffic, past the statue of Joan of Arc, past the Obelisk, over the bridge and on to the Boulevard St. Germain. I can't take it in all at once, it's too much to swallow in one gulp. All I can say is "What a city! What a city!".

Suddenly we stop in front of a hotel – the Grand Hotel de France. She has stayed here, Mona, and seems to know the proprietress. The night porter in his green billiard cloth vest recognizes her, greets her warmly. The luggage is dragged up to our room. Immediately the man goes to the French windows and opens them up. We have a little balcony on the street, rue Bonaparte. As I step out on the balcony the church bells begin to ring. Such a beautiful way to welcome us to Paris.

3

I listen with new ears; it is the first time in my life that the sound of church bells has meant anything to me. Soon there is sound of klaxons, and a fire engine sweeps through the narrow street. Are they real firemen? They look exactly like the ones I played with as a child. What next?

We unpack, wash up, and set out for the boulevard to have a drink. I'm still trembling with excitement. It seems to me that everybody is staring at us. At Mona particularly. Too much make up probably. Or the clothes. Or is it that they see in her something different? We sit down at a little café, not the Deux Magots on the corner.

Mona is talking now — a mile a minute. Giving me the low down on the quartier, pointing out where she ran into this one and that — Borowski, Hemingway, Kokoshka, Tihanyi. Where to eat cheaply when our money begins to give out. Which bookstores are the most exciting. Where one can see Picasso of an evening, or Marcel Duchamp. Where not to go, because there are too many Americans about. Where one can buy African sculpture — or canes such as Borowski sports. How to find one's way around in the Metro. Where the avant-garde films are shown. Which aperitifs are the most pleasant tasting. "Try a Pernod!", she says. I finish my beer and she orders two

Pernods. "How did you say that again?" I'd like at least to be able to order myself a drink when I'm alone. "You can order in English", she says. "Everybody speaks English around here." "But I don't want to ·talk English. I don't want to be taken for an American."

She laughs in my face. "You'll always be an American", she shouts. "Don't try to be anything else. Besides, the French like Americans."

"Good", I said. "So long as they don't take me for a Hun."

The Pernod was wonderful. Seemed to clear my head.

"I wouldn't take another now", said Mona. "Let's eat first. I know a nice little place not far from here — on the rue Jacob. André Gide goes there some times."

I was watching the women passing by as she talked. I hadn't seen a really striking one yet. Most of them seemed rather homely to me, though they carried themselves well.

"We'll go the Brasserie Lipp some time", she was saying. "There you'll meet everyone you've ever heard of. It's ...'"

"Excuse me", I said, "but there's the first stunning-looking one I've seen so far". I indicated a young woman standing at the curb.

"Oh *her!*" she exclaimed. "She's a well-known model. Poses for Soutine, I think, or maybe it's Matisse. Rather fleshy, don't you think? But that's how they like 'em here."

"Looks good to me", I said. "I like a little flesh too."

"I must take you to a whorehouse some time ...'"

"What?"

"Yes, a whorehouse. Women go as well as men, you know. You sit around and drink ... you don't have to go with the girls if you don't want to."

"I'd rather go alone. It sounds crazy to me, dragging your wife to a whorehouse."

"It's fun", she said. 'Everybody does it."

Walking to the restaurant — we made a slight detour so as to take in some of the colorful streets in the neighborhood — my eyes feasted on even the tiniest details. What gorgeous streets for a man striving for something different all his life! The rue de Buci, the rue Mazarine, the rue de Seine: nothing but quaint dilapidated hotels, brilliant awnings, bars, food emporiums, art stores, bookshops, one thing piled on top another, men, women, dogs, cats, lunatics, vegetables, carcasses, bric-a-brac, treasures from Africa and Asia, paintings by poets, pastries by masters, billboards, ensigns, emblems, scarred and charred walls decorated with letters ten feet tall advertising drinks, talcum powders, tires, cheeses, what not.

We sit on the sidewalk, where one did everything apparently, depending on the weather and the time of day. Mona had to explain the various dishes to me. It seemed like an enormous menu — such a variety of meats, vegetables, cheeses, wines, liqueurs, hors d'oeuvres. I let her order for me, astonished to hear her rattle it off in French. I had always been dubious that she knew any French. Her vocabulary wasn't very extensive, I soon discovered, but it was enough to get us by.

What struck me most about that first meal was the animation with which people ate. They ate and talked, and laughed and joked. They not only enjoyed the food, they seemed to enjoy one another's company. Didn't they in America too? Only now and then, it seemed to me. Americans never impressed me as enjoying anything properly.

And they were certainly deficient in the art of conversation. If only I knew what these frogs were talking about! If only I could join in!

"Do you get any of it?" I asked.

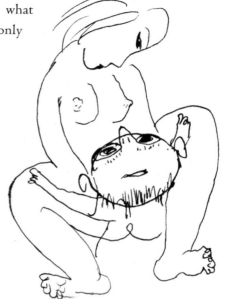

"No, Val, it's too fast for me. Besides, the Parisians use a lot of slang."

"It sure sounds beautiful", I said. "And so much more vigorous than I thought. I used to think it a feminine language, all flowers and perfume."

"Wait till you hear them swear."

"I wouldn't know the difference", I recalled. "By the way, give me a couple of swear words. I'd like to know what it sounds like."

She leaned forward and said with a grin: "*Merde!*"

"What's that mean?"

"Shit. Isn't it lovely?"

"Sounds rather innocuous to me. Can't you give me something stronger?"

"*Vous êtes un con*", she volunteered.

"What's *con?*"

"Actually it means cunt, but when you say *vous êtes un con*, what it really means is — You're a prick!"

"That's a strange one", I said. "So they reverse it here. I must get a dictionary of slang."

"First you'd better get an ordinary one. And a map of the Metro."

"And you write out the names of a few good dishes for me!"

"Listen, Val", she cut in, "Just choose at random. Point with your finger. Everything's good in France. You can't pick a bad dish, even if you try. The same for the wines. They're all marvellous, even the vin ordinaire. Let's go somewhere for a coffee. I'd love a Chartreuse with my coffee. Let's go to the Café Flore – it's not so crowded as some of the others. Or would you like to try Montparnasse – the Dôme, for instance?"

I decided that Montparnasse could wait. "Let's stay in this quarter", I suggested. "Pick any joint you like."

The church bells began ringing again. It was entrancing. Why didn't they sound that way at home?

"Do you remember Huysmans, Val? There's a church a little farther up the street, probably the ugliest in Paris – St. Sulpice. Huysmans wrote about it in *La Bas*. Paris is full of churches. The best one, in my opinion, is St. Chapelle. Next to Chartres I think it the most beautiful in France."

"What about Notre Dame?"

"It's beautiful too, but it doesn't move me. Maybe it's been looked at too much."

As we took a seat on the *terrasse* of the Flore, Mona pointed out this one and that, all celebrities, most of them unknown to me even by name. "Each artist has his own café", she explained. "It's in the café he meets his friends, not at his home. Most of them don't have a home,

anyway; they live in hotel rooms or gar-
rets. If a Frenchman invites you to
his home you can take it
you've made a real friend."

"I like that". I said
promptly. "I means
meeting one's friends
at a café rather than at
home. Privacy is
something we've never
had."

"Yes", said Mona
eagerly, "No one here
thinks of barging in on you
unannounced. They either
telephone or send you a *pneuma-
tique* — that's like a special delivery
letter, only it looks like a telegram."

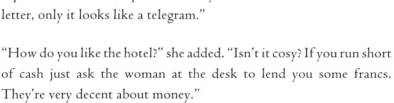

"How do you like the hotel?" she added. "Isn't it cosy? If you run short
of cash just ask the woman at the desk to lend you some francs.
They're very decent about money."

"That doesn't sound French to me", I said.

"You're right. The French are not very generous, on the whole, but
the people at the hotel are different. They come from the Midi, that's
the south of France. Another breed entirely."

"Let's hope we don't run short", said I. "We have enough now to last
us a year, if we don't get reckless."

"That's the trouble", said Mona. "One does get reckless over here. Too much to see, too much to do, too much to buy. You can't resist."

"Well, let's take it easy to begin with. Jesus, I'd be happy if I did nothing more than eat and drink the way we're doing now, and walk the streets and gape and stare."

"We don't want to stay in Paris forever, do we?" said Mona. "There's so much else to see. There's Germany, Austria, Hungary, Poland, Romania ..."

"Hold on! Let's get a taste of Paris first. Don't rush me all over the map right away, *please*. Sure, I want to go places, see things, but not all at once. *Romania*, you say. That's a strange one. Why Romania?"

"Because I have relatives there. I was born in the Carpathians, remember?"

"Where was it again?"

"In Bukovina."

"Okay. We'll go there one day. But not till we've had a good look at France, eh?"

"As you please", she replied. "Only I know *you*. You've got itchy feet."

"I'd like to see the whole wide world, that's what. But you can't do it on a shoestring. If we had the dough. I'd say let's go to India, China, Bali, Persia. I could go on travelling for the rest of my life."

"And what about writing?" she said, with a sly gleam in her eye.

"*That*, there's always time for that. Now we're travelling."

"Couldn't you write too?"

"I don't know. Maybe. We'll see."

"Maybe we'll find just the spot to settle down in, some place where you'd feel at home ... maybe in the south of France."

"I wouldn't care where it was", I replied. "If only we had enough to live on. It would be tough trying to beg in French."

"We're not going to beg", said Mona defiantly. "You're going to write and you're going to get paid for your work. Trust me. I'll take care of all that."

"Let's drop the subject, what do you say? I don't want to think about money any more. Let's just live and forget."

11

The next morning we had breakfast in bed, or rather Mona did. I was already up and dressed, ready to stretch my legs; the bells were ringing again, the air was soft and balmy. Springtime in Paris: the dream of every tourist. The croissants were delicious and the dark chicory-flavoured coffee just to my taste.

"What's the program for today?" I asked, as she made for the bathroom.

"I think we'll go to see Borowski, if you don't mind."

"Just like that? No warning? I thought you had to send a what you call it first."

"Not with Borowski", she replied. "We're old friends."

I waited patiently on the balcony while she made ready to go, always a long procedure with her. What a lively spectacle it was from up there on the third floor: where in America could I look down on a stream of traffic such as this? She had picked a good street for a first taste of Paris. It was alive, intimate, colorful — as gay as the tricolor itself.

"We'll walk there", she said. "It's only a few blocks from here. Near the Luxembourg Gardens. He'll be thrilled."

I wasn't so sure he'd be thrilled to see *me*. From all she had told me about the wonderful days and nights they had spent together, to say nothing of the gifts she had brought back from his studio, I was a bit apprehensive. I tried to convey the thought to her but she dismissed it as absurd. In the past, whenever I had been introduced to one of her lovers — "admirers", she called them — it was never as her husband. I was usually passed off as one of her writer friends. Borowski, she had told me, treated her as a fellow artist, a writer, no less. It would be interesting to know, could I open him up, just what he thought about

her writing. I also wondered what she would say when he inquired about those "gifts" she had taken with her to America.

She pulled the bell rope at the garden door and in a moment there came a man's voice — rather sharp and querulous, I thought — demanding to know who was there.

"It's me, Mona", she said softly.

With that the door was unlocked and there stood Borowski, no mistaking him, pipe in hand, beret cocked jauntily over his thick mop of iron-gray hair.

They embraced warmly and then I was introduced — "my husband". From the fleeting expression that passed over his face I realized that a husband was the last thing he expected her to present him with.

"Come in, come in", he said. "Well, so you're back. And where is Stasia?"

Before she could reply he was leading us toward the huge figures which were standing about. The weather permitting he worked outdoors. He seemed diminutive by comparison with the creations in stone and wood which surrounded him. The words bubbled out of his mouth as he expatiated on each figure in turn. He moved in and out of them rapidly like a squirrel. He talked the same way. And with an air of authority. The vitality which emanated from him was electrifying.

Mona of course was full of admiration for his work. Always lavish with her encomiums, she gushed over each piece as if nothing like it had ever been produced before. Those which she had seen before she went up to and caressed with a display of tenderness which was positively embarrassing.

"You're just in time for lunch", said Borowski, as he excused himself to change his clothes. He and I had hardly exchanged a dozen words, it seemed to me. He reappeared looking raunchy and dapper. Evidently he had his clothes made in England. Everything of the best.

Including the slouch hat which he wore at a rakish angle. At the door of his studio he paused a moment to select a cane; I noticed that there were at least a dozen to choose from, all distinctive and exotic.

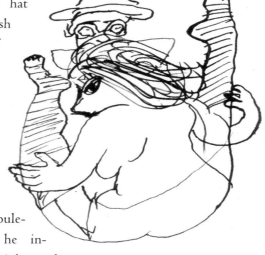

We would eat on the boulevard Montparnasse, he informed us. First a drink at the Select. As we walked he mingled witticisms, stories, observations on this and that, all in rapid fire style. He was a ball of fire, no doubt about it. And a formidable adversary if one had to lock horns with him. Now and then he would shoot a question about Stasia, but hardly seemed to listen to Mona's replies.

We sat down on the *terrasse* of the Select, which was already quite crowded. He nodded to various friends, shook hands with one or two, then asked us what we would like to drink.

"Pernod", said I, without stopping to think.

"No!" he said. "Let me order something more interesting. Anybody can drink Pernod. It's vile". He called for Saint Raphael – three of them.

"I suppose you're a writer too", he said, suddenly addressing me.

Mona immediately explained that I was the writer she had told him about when she was here last year.

15

"Yes, yes, of course", he said. "You're all writers in America, aren't you?" He followed this up with some flippant remark about what a strange country America was. Adding that we were really becoming a pest to the European. "I suppose you will settle down and take a studio, is that it? Write the great American novel, that sort of thing." With this a few words in French which he addressed to the air.

I felt too slow-witted to cope with these remarks. I simply grinned and sipped my Raphael.

"You must meet Calder some time", he said.

"Who's Calder?" I asked.

At this Borowski threw his head back and gave a loud guffaw. "How American! So you don't know who Calder is! ... Well, you'll find out soon enough."

"Of course you know him", said Mona. "You've seen his mobiles, I'm sure."

"Oh, that guy", I said. "Of course I know who you mean, But I never met him."

"How about Hemingway?" I shook my head. "Steinbeck'? Dos Passos?"

"Just names to me", I confessed.

I assumed that this finished me in Borowski's eyes. It was hard to tell what he thought about anything or anybody; he had a malicious tongue and he knew how to use it. If some one came over to shake hands with him he would jump up like a Jack-in-the-Box, exchange a few words. and then as he resumed his seat he would remark with contempt or disdain: "An impossible chap ... a bore". Only in French it sounded worse because with everything he disliked he had to say it

was *"emmerdant"*. He was highly irascible too. Forever bawling the waiters out, annoyed when people brushed his shoulder in slipping by the table. Yet withal jovial, witty, always animated, always darting, bounding, pouncing.

We had lunch on the sidewalk outside some modest restaurant where we wouldn't be molested, as he said. As usual, he decided what we would eat and drink, with considerable snapping of the fingers and banging of the table for attention. As he ate he dished out little anecdotes about his friends, his ordeals as a novice, between whiles recommending a film or a play that we must not fail to see. His talk fascinated me despite an innate dislike which I tried to suppress. He spoke with an accent, whether speaking English or French. But it was an accent which enhanced his words. Often he invented a word, if the right one didn't come to mind immediately. A charming fellow, as my friend Stanley used to say.

"Isn't he wonderful?" said Mona as we were walking back to the hotel. "I told you you'd like him. And he's a very great sculptor too ... better than Rodin by far. He's very sensitive, perhaps because of his size.

That's what makes him so cocky and aggressive. But he doesn't mean anything by it. He's a good friend. You can count on him." She paused a moment. "And he likes you too, though he tried to hide it."

"Jealous, no doubt", said I.

We were walking through the Luxembourg Gardens, past the Queens of France. "There's nothing like this anywhere", said Mona. "Stasia and I used to come here often to eat our lunch. He liked Stasia very much."

"Who did?"

"Borowski. He said she had enormous talent — but no discipline. He teaches, you know, in some Academy. I forget the name now. I used to go with Stasia and watch her work."

She went on and on about Stasia, the artists they had met, their outings in the Bois de Boulogne, the *bals musette*, the flea market, the Hotel Princesse where they lived without a cent for three weeks, and so on. I only half listened. I was thinking how strange it was that the first Frenchman, the first European I should meet was this famous sculp-

tor, Borowski. Had I met
Rodin or Bourdelle, would
it have gone off so easy? I
wondered vaguely if I
would get to know
Marcel Duchamp, or
even André Gide.
Too late, alas, to
know Apollinaire or
Modigliani.

"Did you ever meet
Cocteau?" I asked.

"Yes, of course", she said.
"But he's seldom here, he
lives in the south of France somewhere."

"Did you ever hear of a place called *Le Rat Mort*?"

"I think so. Why? Why do you ask?"

"Oh, it's one of those places I'd like to see sometime. Many famous
men used to gather there ... Cezanne, for instance, George Moore,
Zola, Rimbaud ..."

"Rimbaud?"

"Yes, and Verlaine too, probably."

"I wish I had known that, Val. Stasia would go crazy to see that place.
Because of Rimbaud, if nothing else."

"We'll look it up sometime."

19

As we reached the hotel she said, "Wait a minute, let's cross the street. I want to show you a little street where Balzac had his printing shop." She steered me to the rue Visconti. "And on the next block, I think it is, Oscar Wilde used to live. Oh yes, and I forgot to tell you when we were at Borowski's that right near there Strindberg used to live. There's a plaque outside the hotel giving the date."

"Who hasn't lived here at some time or other?" I said to myself.

We strode back to the hotel to take a nap. The day was young yet. When the bells began to ring it would be time for an aperitif. I preferred Pernod to the Raphael; it put lead in your pencil.

It was hard to get to sleep immediately. Seemed to me the room smelled musty. How many thousands of people had slept in this room, I wondered. Everything looked worn, worn but clean. The big mirror showed streaks of quicksilver — too many people had stared into it. But what a comfortable bed! One drowned in it. I opened the little compartment in the night table just to see. Sure enough, there was a pisspot standing there. That and the bidet — indispensable. As for the bath, that was down the hall somewhere. You had to notify the maid when you wanted to take one. You paid extra for it too. You paid for soap and matches also, I noticed. And whatever you did always involved a tip. Even when you went to the toilet in a café. I didn't mind; it seemed rather cute. Kept money in circulation. If by paying extra we could have had some decent towels I would have ordered some. According to Mona, there were no other kind; only when you took a bath could you have a Turkish towel. Besides, you had to use your towels discreetly; they didn't change them every day, as in America.

The sound of the bells woke me up. I dashed to the balcony to hear them better. Again the fire engines passed. Must have a lot of fires in Paris. Or maybe they were just practising. Anyway, looking up and down the street, I was entranced by the milk and gray aspect of the walls. And what huge doorways! What locks and bolts! And the iron shutters that were rolled down at close of day. When they closed down they closed down here. *Fermé*. No two ways about it.

This time we took a seat at the corner, just a block below the Deux Magots. There was hardly room between the tables and the gutter for a pedestrian to pass. We ordered our Pernod and settled down to observe the scene. Just as the waiter appeared Mona caught sight of a man crossing the street; his back was toward us. She jumped up and ran after him. He flung his arms around her and kissed her. She dragged him back to the café.

"This is Michonze", she said, putting an arm around his shoulder. "He's the poorest painter in all Paris. And the greatest friend any one could ask for. Sit down, have a drink with us!"

"With pleasure", he said, in perfect English. "So you got married in the meantime? Congratulations!"

"We've been married for years", said Mona. "Only I never told you."

He smiled and said: "Isn't she wonderful? Always up to some new trick. How long are you staying? I'd like to show you what I've done since you left. It's not much, of course … you know what my life is. Still, I manage to knock out a painting now and then."

21

"Of course we want to see your work", said Mona. "Don't we, Val? One day you're going to be famous."

"One day", he echoed. "If I live that long." With this he began talking about Modigliani, whom he had known, and Soutine, whom he spoke of as a pal. Soutine was doing well now, but in bad health. Too much carousing, too much starvation. Max Ernst's name was on his lips. Another good friend. They had been through the worst together."

"What about Reichel?" said Mona. "And Tihanyi? Are they still around?"

"Why not?" he said. "You can't kill them off as easily as that."

"Where did you learn English?" I asked after a while. "You seem to speak it perfectly."

"English! That came easy. I learned it from you Americans. It's the Americans who keep me alive. Ask Mona." He went on to say that languages came easy to him; he knew six or seven at least. He turned to Mona. "You know whom I can't understand even to this day? He drives me crazy too. *Tihanyi.*" He explained to me that Tihanyi was a Hungarian who was deaf. A good painter too. He taught himself to learn French and English, German too ... perhaps other languages, who knows? But since he couldn't hear his own words he had no idea what his French or English sounded like. It was absolutely atrocious, a sort of baboon's tongue. "And if you understand him he gets angry."

"It's true", said Mona. "But he's adorable. You can't help liking him with all his faults. I always pretend to understand. But sometimes that makes him angry too."

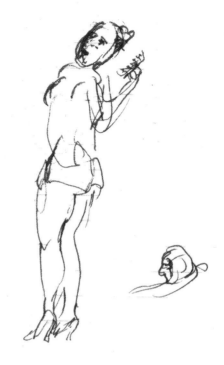

"And how is Stasia?" asked Michonze.

"She's fine", Mona replied.

"Where is she now?"

"I don't know. Maybe she's here in Paris."

She quickly changed the subject. "Why don't we go and have a look at your paintings? Maybe you'd like to have dinner with us?"

"Excellent", said Michonze. "If we have time I'll do a portrait of you."

"In that case I'll run back to the hotel", said Mona, "and put on my velvet cape and my hat that Val likes so much."

She was back in a jiffy and off we started to Michonze's *atelier*. It was on the rue Vaugirard, top floor. A foul, smelly building, dark as a prison. He didn't even have a room; his *atelier* was the bit of hallway from the stairs to the W.C. Just big enough for a cot, a chair and a table. By the light of a dim electric bulb we inspected his work. I didn't know what to make of the canvases; all I could think of was that they reminded me of Russia and Poland where he had come from originally.

Soon he was busy making Mona's portrait. He was especially captivated by the hat; he seemed to concentrate on that rather than her face. It took him only about three-quarters of an hour to complete the job. It was a good likeness and rather flattering. Mona thought it wonderful. "I'm taking it", she said, and with that drew a fifty dollar bill from her purse. I thought she was being rather stingy, but Michonze appeared to think it more than adequate. "Maybe I'll be able to get out of this place now", he said, stuffing the bill in his pocket. "Let me take you people to dinner!" We wouldn't hear of that, naturally. "Well then, let me *give* you a painting." He dragged out some canvases from under the cot. "Choose anything you like", he said.

It took her another twenty minutes to decide which one she preferred. Finally he said: "Let's get out of here. You can come back another day and pick one out. The portrait has to dry first anyway."

He selected a modest restaurant on the rue de Seine, a place where students ate. It was gay, noisy, and the food was excellent. He promised to give us the addresses of similar restaurants so that we wouldn't waste our money.

We sauntered slowly back to Montparnasse and again installed ourselves on the *terrasse* of the Select. Hardly had we taken our seats when some one slapped me on the back, saying: "*Miller*, how *are* you? My God, how did *you* get here?" I looked up and so help me if it

wasn't my old friend Johnny
Dunn of the Cosmodemonic
Telegraph days.

"Sit down", I said, "and
have a drink with us." I
presented him to
Michonze and to Mona.

"This is the man who first
told me about Rimbaud", I
said to Mona. "I've told you
about him often, don't you remember? How he met his for-
mer boss outside the Flatiron
Building one day while working as a
messenger and the next week he was in the Queen of
Romania's winter palace in the Carpathians."

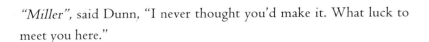

"*Miller*", said Dunn, "I never thought you'd make it. What luck to
meet you here."

"I never would have made it", said I, "if it weren't for her", nodding
toward Mona.

"You don't have to tell me", he said, with a twinkle in his eye. "Let
me congratulate you." He turned to Mona. "What an extraordinary
voice you have", he said. "Are you an actress by chance?"

"I was once", said Mona. "Not much of a one though."

"I would say you could be a very great actress", said Dunn. He turned
to me. "I have a friend with me ... over there", he said, pointing to a
table nearby. "We're going to the theatre tonight. Could I invite you
to come with your wife?"

"Is it in English?" I asked.

"No, it's in French. A farce, with Max Dearly. I don't suppose you know his name. I'm crazy about him."

Mona immediately decided against it. "But you go, Val", she urged. "You'll enjoy it."

I decided I would. It was getting late for the theatre. We collected his lady friend and hopped a cab.

"Miller", he said, "you don't know what a lucky man you are. To have a wife like that — it's incredible. And what a voice! Every time she opens her mouth I feel as if I were going to have an ejaculation. I wouldn't leave a woman like that alone for two minutes ... in Paris ... or anywhere ... if I were in your boots."

"And what are you doing here?" I asked. "I thought you lived in Scheveningen, or is it the Hague?"

"I do", he said. "We're having a little vacation. We're leaving for the country in a few days. Maybe you'd like to join us. Have you learned any French yet?"

"I only arrived yesterday", I said. "Or was it the day before? Seems like I've been here a week already."

"I hope you stay here", he said. "Don't ever go back to America. What a dreadful place! I never was so miserable in my life as in New York. Thanks to you I got out alive."

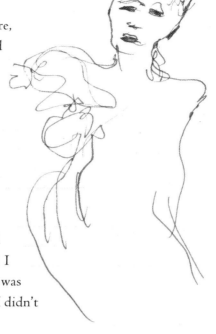

We pulled up at the theatre, bought another ticket and rushed in. The curtain was just going up. "Don't try to understand the words", he whispered, as we took our seats. "Just look!' I'll explain it all to you later."

It was a bedroom farce, as best I remember, with nothing to recommend it except Max Dearly whom every one seemed to think was delicious. I had all I could do, by the time the play was half over, to keep my eyes open. I didn't understand a word.

He drove me back to the hotel immediately after the show; we agreed to meet again in a day or two. The woman he called his mistress had hardly breathed a word. She was half Dutch, half Javanese, he said. "And wonderful in bed", he whispered. I never did find out what the play was about.

Mona was creaming her face as I walked in. I was rather surprised that she was back so early. "You must have been bored", I said.

"God, no! I had a marvellous time. You had hardly left when Varese appeared, then Kokoschka, and finally Marcel Duchamp. The conversation was just marvellous ..."

"In what language?" I asked.

"In English. They all speak English, except Vlaminck. He can speak it too, I'm sure, but he didn't want to ..."

"And how was the play? Did you enjoy it?"

"I fell asleep in the last act."

"I'll take you to the *Grand Guignol* some night. I'll guarantee you won't fall asleep there. By the way, what does your friend do now? He's a rather strange person, I thought."

"How do you mean?"

"Rather degenerate, if you ask me."

"I wouldn't say *that*. Certainly he's been around, seen everything, tried everything. A man of the world, you might say. I learned a lot from him. He's one of the reasons I'm here, I guess."

"Does he write or paint?"

"No, he doesn't have to. He just lives. Speaks about nine languages you know. Including Bulgarian, Serbian and Arabic. No Hungarian, though. I can still see the two of us hanging on to a strap in the subway and him telling me about writers like Apollinaire, Gottfried Benn, Paul Valery, Max Jacob. He has a wonderful gift for describing places too. And what places! He's lived in almost every capital of the world and he knows them inside out. It all started with the war and his ability to memorize lengthy documents which he carried in his noodle from one country to another. He knows a bit about art as well. That's how

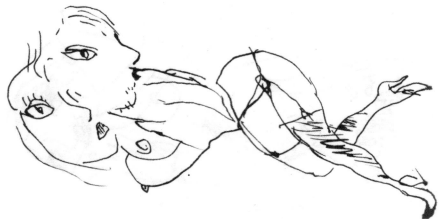

he came to America, if you remember. He was trying to unload a case of precious masterpieces and got caught with his pants down. It was a lucky day for me when he came to my office to ask for a messenger job. That wife of mine couldn't stand him, of course. He was too sophisticated, too cynical, she said. But then she never did like any of my friends, unless it was Ulric. Wouldn't it be wonderful if *he* were to show up here one day, the bugger?"

"I certainly hope we don't run into your friend MacGregor. I can't stand that man."

"Christ, I forgot all about *him*. He's about due now, isn't he? That is, if he went through with his plan. I wonder how he made out with that gal of his."

"Val, if we run into him I'm walking away. I don't see how you put up with him all these years."

"We're going to run into a lot of people we don't want to meet, I'm afraid. Especially if we go to the Dôme. That's the first place they head for, isn't it?"

"Michonze virtually lives there", said Mona. "He's there day and night, he tells me."

"When does he paint then?"

"That's it, *when?* He's only one of thousands who spend the whole day searching for a meal. That's why I bought the portrait. He may not sell another painting for six months."

"Well, if one has to starve I think I'd rather starve here than anywhere else. At least there are benches to sit down on once in a while. And if you have the price of a coffee you can go to a café and keep warm. You can even write your letters there, I notice."

"Let's not talk about starving, Val. Time enough for that when we get home."

As we climbed into bed I asked if she had heard from Pop yet.

"How could I? We have to go to the American Express for our mail. Maybe we'll go tomorrow. Then I can show you the Palais Royal, the Tuileries, and the rue de la Paix."

"Fuck the rue de la Paix! I'm not buying any jewellery yet. I'd rather see Les Halles or Notre Dame. Or what's that church you were raving about ... Ste. Chapelle, was-it?"

"Yes, yes. Ste, Chapelle. By all means let's go there tomorrow. You'll never see the like of it again. It takes your breath away. We should go to the bird market too; it's not far from there."

"Okay", I said. "But one of these days I intend to take a stroll all by my lonesome. It'll be fun to get lost in a city like this."

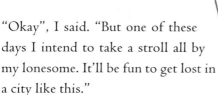

31

Part Two

So it began. We must have covered a good part of Paris on foot in those first few days. The walk to the American Express, which was to be repeated many times, was an act of discovery. So much to see, so much to be thankful for. Every day, I said to myself: "Thank God from whom all blessings flow!" As for Pop, each day I begged God to enfold him in "his savin' and keepin' power".

The quarter I immediately fell in love with was around the Place Contrescarpe. The rue Mouffetard particularly. Everything about it, including the outlandish baths at the foot of the street, reminded me of the East Side, the ghetto: Orchard, Delancey, Allen streets. A world of edibles and of people who appreciated them. Eat, drink and be merry! Each vegetable had a beauty and a life of its own. Even the pigs hanging on the hooks looked ravishing. So clean and pink, so enticing with the shamrock stuck in one ear. The Latin Quarter was interesting too, but in a totally different way. What a street, the rue Monsieur le Prince, with its exotic restaurants, its bookstores and shabby *hotels de passe*. Or the rue Champollion, the very name of which conjured up magic. But why enumerate or specify? Every street, *place, impasse, ruelle* or boulevard was a world in itself. Behind the high walls there was still another world. Whenever I looked at the map of Paris I was reminded of the human brain with its convolutions of gray matter.

Only, through the city of Paris there ran that romantic artery called the Seine, without which Paris would cease to be Paris.

For some reason which I never understood we were always having our aperitifs and our meals on the Left Bank. Only once, in those early days, did we venture up to Montmartre. Evidently Mona hadn't spent much time up there on her last trip. Though she pretended to find it quaint and charming I could see that she preferred other sections of the city. Myself I was somewhat disappointed in Montmartre. I had expected something else, something more authentic. It smacked somewhat of Greenwich Village, I thought. No doubt there were great painters living here still but their work wasn't much in evidence. I tried in vain to summon the spirit which once animated it – in the days of Utrillo, Van Gogh, Francis Carco and such like. No, we were more at home in St. Germain and Montparnasse. As for the Champs-Elysees, it left me cold. The *grands boulevards* appealed to me more. One could still find traces there of the atmosphere which the Impressionists had captured in their paintings.

It was inevitable that we should run into Tihanyi. By six o'clock he was sure to be installed on the *terrasse* of the Dôme, usually surrounded by fawning females. My first brush with him brought back Michonze's words. He was not only irascible but an unholy bore, a crapulous one at that. Mona thought he was irresistible. It's true, if one wanted to know what was going on in Paris all one had to do was ask Tihanyi. He was like a receiving and sending station. He read a dozen different papers a day and all the revues he could lay hands on, in addition to which he had the faculty of picking things out of the air. Should you drop the name of an artist he would give you an evaluation of his work in less time than it takes to run up the Union Jack.

His estimate of a fellow artist was generally negative, expressed by a deprecating grimace which was only a shade more sour than his customary look. It was hard to tell whether this look was due to his affliction or his turn of mind. When he smiled or grinned, he looked the clown. But he was forever griping about something, if only the weather, and in a language which no one could understand, even a Hungarian. If he wished to make a telephone call he would ask someone to accompany him to the booth in order to call the number; once he got his party he dropped the receiver and just spouted. There was no chance for the one at the other end to respond. He simply said his say and hung up. Evidently it worked.

I was much more interested in a man seated against the big pane of glass in the rear of the *terrasse*. This strange individual was bobbing up and down in a state of agitation, signalling to this one and that as they passed. Obviously he was half crocked. His smile was like a frog's greeting the dawn, a truly wonderful smile which seemed to embrace the animate and the inanimate world. Now and then he waved his arms ecstatically or held his hat high above his head, as if saluting the flag. Having caught sight of Mona talking to Tihanyi he now endeavored to induce her, by means of strange signals and grimaces, to drop Tihanyi and join him.

"Who is that guy?" I finally asked.

"That's Reichel, Val. I'll see him in a minute. He's drunk now and happy, for a while. But he'll soon change. We'll say hello to him and run off. Otherwise we'll never get rid of him."

It was not so easy however to unlatch Tihanyi. He wanted to talk, wanted to hear about New York, wanted to know if she had looked up his Hungarian friends as she had promised. He also wanted to know, as I gathered from the notes he scribbled, what she had done with the paintings he had lent her to show the New York art dealers. She wriggled out of it by excusing herself to run to the lavatory. Left alone with him I made no attempt to carry on a conversation. He tried handing me notes, but I pretended I couldn't understand his handwriting. That disgusted him. He gave me a sour look, took up the newspaper beside him and began reading it.

Mona returned to her seat just as Reichel decided to join us. Rising to his feet, he lurched forward, bumping into waiters, tables, spilling drinks, losing his hat, and apologizing for the curses which were being hurled at him from every direction. With his hat awry, his arms waving frantically, his face beaming like the harvest moon, he was indeed a sight. All the while he kept babbling in French and German, as if he were alone in his room reciting a passage from the Nibelungen Lied. Finally, like a wreck thrown up on a coral strand, he managed to reach our table, and with one fell swoop he pounced on Mona and embraced her like a long lost sister. To me he addressed some unintelligible words in his own drunken language and proceeded to wring my hand as if it were a dinner bell he was clutching. He was no longer half crocked; he was now completely *schlass*.

"Cigarette!" he mumbled, fluttering his fingers in my face.

I handed him a Camel which he took one look at and threw to the ground. "He wants a Gauloise", said Mona. Whereupon Reichel spluterringly repeated – "*Gauloise, ja! Kein Camelle.*" With this he

threw in what sounded like a few healthy
oaths from the potato fields of
Pomerania, then smiled an-
gelically, threw his arms
around me and kissed
me on both cheeks.

Tihanyi meanwhile
had fled.

Fortunately for us a
friend of Reichel's
soon came along and
carried him off. He was
still waving his arms and
protesting vigorously as he
rounded the corner.

"He's a wonderful person", said Mona,
as we started across the street. "You'll enjoy talking with him when
he's sober. I want you to see his work some day. His watercolors are
like jewels. People say that he imitates Paul Klee, who was once a great
friend of his, but it isn't true. There are resemblances, of course."

As we passed the Rotonde Borowski called to us. He looked as dapper
as ever and seemed genuinely pleased to run into us. I noticed that he
was sporting another of his exotic canes, an African one this time.

We had a drink or two and then he proposed that we drop into a dance
place on the opposite corner. It was a typical Montparnasse joint, full
of whores, and very crowded. It seemed a delightful place to me until
my head began to spin.

The next evening, as we were going up the rue Delambre, we ran
straight into that Austrian whom Mona pretended to hate, the one

who was in love with Stasia. Carl was his name. As it was raining, we decided to go back to the Dôme. I liked Carl immediately. After a drink or two I noticed that Mona didn't hate him as much as she had pretended. They had it out about Stasia, whom he declared he still loved madly, and then the talk drifted to books and writing. He was very curious about America, having had several American mistresses, he confessed. Could I tell him something about the Wild West, about Arizona particularly? Another drink and he was begging us to take him back with us. He liked New York too. he said. Maybe he could find a job as a waiter or a barman there.

"But you're a writer, aren't you?" I asked.

He smiled sheepishly and said that he had done nothing of importance so far. "Who wants to read German?" Apparently he had written several novels in that language. But now he was writing French. "And maybe", he added, "I will try writing English soon. How do I talk? Do I sound like a Hun?"

I thought he had a very good command of English. "The accent doesn't matter", I said. "In New York nobody talks good English."

"I've met some American writers here", he said, "but I didn't care much for them. You're different. You talk like Sherwood Anderson."

"Did you meet *him*?" I asked enthusiastically. "He's one of my favorite writers, you know. I never met him, of course. I don't think I know any American writer personally. Unless it's Maxwell Bodenheim."

"You'll meet plenty of them here", said Carl. "Hemingway, Dos Passos, Cummings, Gertrude Stein."

"I'm not eager to meet any of them", I said. "I'd rather meet French writers."

That obviously pleased him. He didn't
know many of them himself, he admit-
ted. "I'm too shy. Besides, I have nothing to say."

"I'd love to meet Tristan Tzara,
or Louis Aragon — or wait a
minute ... did you ever hear of
a writer called Blaise Cendrars?"

It was Cendrars' name which really
started us off, I believe. He was surprised that I had ever heard of him.
Asked if I had ever read *Moravagine.* I
explained that scarcely anything of his had
been translated into English. Then I went on to tell him of my love
for Marcel Proust, Thomas Mann, André Gide — and Anatole France.
At the mention of the last named he made a face.

"What's the matter?" I asked.

He laughed. "All you Americans seem crazy about Anatole France. Or
else it's Flaubert, Zola, Baudelaire, de Maupassant. You're fifty years
behind."

"Well, what about American literature? Who do you like among
American authors? Edgar Allen Poe, I suppose."

"Sure I do", said Carl. "What's wrong with *him?*"

"Nothing, I suppose, only he leaves me cold."

"I like Jack London too", said Carl.

"Who doesn't? Even the Chinese love Jack London."

"Tell him about Elie Faure", said Mona.

"Who's that?" said Carl.

"What?" she exclaimed. "You don't know the man who wrote the *History of Art?*"

"In what language?" said Carl.

"In French, of course. What did you think he was, a Turk?"

"Never heard of him", said Carl. "I'll tell you who I do like, though", he added. Walt Whitman! I've read him in German, French and English. He's marvellous in any language."

That brought us to Emerson, Thoreau, Melville, Hawthorne. He didn't care much for Emerson or Hawthorne, but Melville he thought great.

"I can't stick him", I confessed. "I tried three times to read *Moby Dick*, but couldn't swallow it. Same for Stendhal. I don't even care much for Baudelaire, to tell the truth."

"You're a strange American", said Carl. "What about *Uncle Tom's Cabin? Garçon!* What about another Pernod?"

"So you like Thomas Mann?" he said, sipping his Pernod. "I suppose you fell in love with Tonio Kruger?"

"I certainly did", I said. "And with Herr Peeperkorn, remember him?"

He laughed again. "I've never met an American who hasn't read *The Magic Mountain*. Frankly, Mann bores me. So does Romain Rolland whom you mentioned a while back. The truth is we have no very great writers today ... in *any* language."

"That's saying a great deal", I said. "There's always one great writer at least in every epoch."

"Maybe you're the great writer ... *to come*", said Carl.

"I haven't even begun", I said.

"That's not true", said Mona. "He's written reams of stuff already, including two novels." As usual she began to build me up. Carl listened seriously, as seriously as he was capable of listening to such nonsense.

When she had finished he turned to me and said: "I'm sure you can do as well as Dos Passos or even Sherwood Anderson."

"What do you know about me, my ability?" I said jeeringly.

"I can tell from the way you talk. You're not an Ezra Pound, that's certain. Nor a T.S. Eliot, nor a Henry James. You're a writer, I'm positive of it. I wish you'd let me see some of your work some time. Will you?"

I blushingly confessed that I had nothing to show.

"Well, write something then! No, don't. I'd rather take you on faith. Show me something five years from now, or ten, what difference does it make?"

41

Mona excused herself to go to the lavatory. Carl looked at me with a curious gleam in his eye and said: "I've already read you, you know". I was about to protest, but he put up his hand. "You don't fool me, nor she either. That stuff she showed me last year ... those essays and stories ... *you* wrote them, not her! She doesn't fool me one bit. *You're* the writer, not her. She's an actress. Better off stage than on, I'd guess."

I refused to commit myself, but he saw that he had me.

"What I like about you", he said, "is that you're naif, gullible, believing. You're a real American. I mean it as a compliment, not a reproach. The Americans I meet over here — like Bob McAlmon, for instance — bore the shit out of me. They're all would-be writers. Some of them have talent, sure, but they're all lightweights. They want to go bohemian. You're from New York, you say, or Brooklyn. You must have rubbed elbows with Europeans, perhaps in the ghetto. You're slightly tainted already ... in a good way, I mean. You love Europe. You've always loved Europe. Like I love America. You should stick to your writing, even if it isn't any good. You'll never be an Anatole France, thank God! Or a Marcel Proust, for that matter. You're somewhere between Melville and Walt Whitman, I feel. Or between Gorki and Dostoievsky."

Here I stopped him. "Dostoievsky! Christ, if I could come anywhere near him I'd be in seventh heaven. I didn't tell you, did I, that I've read more Russian literature than Anglo Saxon? I'm at home in Russian literature. I even feel like a Russian, at times. But it's easy to love the Russian writers. They're so human, so earthy ..."

"And so mad!" said Carl. "That's what I detect in *you*. You're slightly mad. I could read it between the lines of your stories. You don't get anywhere. You never will. You shouldn't try to write novels. I don't know what you should try ... maybe plays. But don't worry about plot and that sort of thing."

"You know another writer I forgot to mention?" I said. "He's had more influence on me than any one, with the exception of Dostoievsky, I guess."

"Who's that? Wait! Let me guess!"

I sat back and waited while he ran over the likely candidates in his mind.

Suddenly he said: "Rabelais!"

"Awfully close. Yes, I owe a lot to Rabelais. But it's not him I had in mind."

"It isn't Goethe, that's for sure", said Carl.

"How would you know? I read a lot of Goethe ... once upon a time."

"I give up", he said.

" Knut Hamsun!"

He almost let out a shout. "I was going to mention his name, but then I took it back. Of course I can see why you love him. So do I. Or rather, I did. I haven't read anything of his for ages now, it seems."

At this point Mona returned and, hearing Hamsun's name being bandied about, went into a dithyramb on her own. "Sometimes", nodding in my direction, "he makes me feel that I'm living with Knut Hamsun", she said. "One day he's Glahn the hunter, the next Herr Nagel ..."

"Nagel! That's the character I was trying to name", said Carl, his eyes glistening with tears. "I'd rather be Herr Nagel any day than Julien Sorel or even a Martin Eden."

"What about Alyosha?" This from Mona.

"Did you ever see an Austrian who might be an Alyosha?" he sneered. "I'm closer to Mephistopheles than Alyosha."

He hung his head a minute or two, a characteristic gesture of his which indicated that he had said something stupid, then looked up and spoke. Again his eyes were glistening, as if unable to control his emotion. It was quite a long speech, which was unusual for him, as I later discovered. It began with the story of his love for an American girl whom he had met while running a bar. She was the best of all the Americans he had run into and she hailed from New Jersey. She had a little income and she had taken care of him for a while. And then she was called back home.

"And then", Mona interrupted, "you met Stasia".

"Stasia wasn't a girl", said Carl, nor a woman either. Something between an angel and a genius — with lovely breasts."

"Let's skip it", said Mona.

He seemed perfectly willing to drop the subject of Stasia. He had other more important things to relate. What he was trying to tell me was how he came to fall in love with America. "It began with Fenimore Cooper", he said, "whom I read in English. I had a governess as a child

and I had to speak English with her. In Berlin I picked up more English. When the war ended and I got out of the insane asylum ..."

"What?" I exclaimed.

"Yeah, the insane asylum. I'll tell you about that some other time ... What was I saying? Shit, it doesn't matter. You see, soon after I fell in love with Russian literature I came upon your American writers ... Whitman, Melville, Sherwood Anderson ... oh yeah, and another one, a strange bird ... Ambrose Bierce. Do you know his name?"

I nodded. "Go on. Sure I know Ambrose Bierce."

"I don't know how to explain it to you", he continued. "It was like those cocktails I used to mix for your drunken compatriots. I'd try out all sorts of concoctions on them; they didn't know the difference.

Somehow America is like that to me ... a mixture of everything under the sun. Nobody can give you a clear picture of America or her people, especially not an American. The best ones, I find, are the uneducated ones. The simple people — from the sticks, as you say. We don't breed anything like that here in Europe. We're all corrupt, degenerate, poisoned. Sometimes, when I'm with Americans, I think I'm with some strange breed of animal, a cross between a deer and a coyote. You're all so trusting and naive, so willing to help, so generous and forgiving. But not like children either. And at bottom you're all Europeans ... that's the funny part of it. But there's a difference in specific gravity. You may be lacking in culture — what *we* call culture — but you're not lacking in intelligence. You put your intelligence to other purposes. There's not much difference, when you talk, whether you're talking machines or books. You live on some other level. You live in the herd, whereas we live as individuals. But that's what makes you interesting. Take Jack London, for instance. There's a resemblance between Jack London's work and Gorki's, isn't there? But there's also an immense difference. The Americans have a lot in common with the Russians — the 19th Century Russians, I mean. But Russia gave us Tolstoy and Dostoievsky, while America gave Whitman and Melville ... Maybe I'm talking rubbish. But you see what I mean. Certainly Russia could never have produced a Dickens. But I prefer Gogol to Dickens. Yet Dostoievsky thought Dickens was great, did you know that? And Goethe admired Lord Byron ... Where are we, anyhow?"

"Excuse me, I said, "but getting back to Fenimore Gooper, didn't the Germans produce a sort of Fenimore Cooper?"

"You mean Karl May. Sure, I read him too when I was a kid. They also produced a Gottfried Benn, but for him you have no equivalent in America."

He paused again and hung his head. Then he rattled on about the great American scene, for which no novel could ever be written. "I'd like to live there a few years", he said, "and travel all over the country. I'd like to live with the Indians — the Navajos especially — go to places like San Antonio, Medicine Hat, the Badlands of Dakota, the bayou country in Louisiana, the Ozarks in Arkansas, the Grand Canyon ... Even Omaha, Nebraska ... ."

I had to laugh. "That girl of yours sure wised you up."

"I didn't get it from her", he replied. "I got it from reading, and from the cinema. Tom Mix, Bill Hart, Lon Chaney, Charlie Chaplin. We know them all. We adore them."

"I'm afraid", said I, "you won't find their America any more."

"I'm not so sure about that", he said. "They didn't *invent* America, did they?"

"Damned near", I replied. "An America at any rate that most of us never knew, except from history books and legends."

"Well, no matter", said Carl. "There must be something left of the real America. A little of it would go a long way with me. I need it. I'm sick of European literature; it's too manufactured. We need to be de-cultured. We need a breath of fresh air. Or maybe we need another war. We're so civilized that we can't live for long without war. That horrifies you, I suppose. But then you'd have to live here ten or fifteen years before you'd understand. We're full of problems ... insoluble problems. War doesn't solve them either, of course, but it changes the atmosphere. After each war or revolution we produce a crop of interesting writers. For one genius in the realm of art that you produce we produce a dozen. Europe is rotting with geniuses. I'm against genius." Here he laughed at himself and took another swig of Pernod. "It's the Pernod talking", he resumed. "It's vile stuff but it clears the brain, loosens the tongue, makes you forget all the unpleasant things in life. You prefer whisky, I suppose."

"No, I don't. I hate the stuff. I like wine, French wines."

"Good", said Carl. "I'm a bit of a connoisseur. I'll teach you how to drink good French wine."

It was getting late and Mona was restless, wanted to go back to the hotel.

"All right", said Carl, "but what about tomorrow? Tomorrow's my day off. Why don't we meet for lunch?"

"Why not take our lunch and eat in the Luxembourg Gardens?" said Mona.

"Okay", said Carl. "But you bring the lunch, eh? I'll bring the wine."

"That reminds me", I said as we were shaking hands, "did you ever read Remy de Gourmont? Just before we left I was reading his *Night In the Luxembourg*."

He gave me a smile which meant — he's old hat too. He accompanied us to our hotel and, as we were saying good-night, he promised that he would hang on to us like a leech.

"I certainly like that fellow", I said, as we entered our room. "How could you ever have disliked him?"

"I don't any more", said Mona. "But he played me a dirty trick …"

"You mean with Stasia?"

"Yes. He's a little mad, too. Or maybe I should say irrespon- sible, unreliable. He means well but he doesn't follow through. He's weak and fickle."

"He'll have to go some to be more unreliable than us", I remarked calmly. She winced at this.

"You're always making us out to be heartless and treacherous. Why? I don't understand."

"Well, aren't we? Why don't you face facts?"

"Oh, stop it, please! You seem to enjoy running yourself into the ground."

"I guess you're right. Anyway, it was a pleasure to meet your friend Carl. I think we have something in common. It was sure funny to hear him talk about America. What a surprise he'll get, if he ever makes it."

"You never can tell, Val. Some of them find America a wonderful place. It *is* a different world, you can't deny that."

"I'll take him to Arizona some day ... when I'm rich and successful. I wonder if he's ever stood next to a horse or a cow."

We met the next day for lunch, armed with bread, butter, salami, lachs, cheese, olives, fruit. Carl had three bottles of wine with him: an Aloxe-Corton, a Gevrey-Chambertin and a Nuit St. Georges, or perhaps it was a Pommard. We took a seat near the pond where the

49

kids sail their boats. The Queens of France surrounded us. The trees were in full bloom. It was a heavenly day and nothing to mar our pleasure. Carl was in form, delighted with the food we had brought, and in love with the wines he had chosen. He even tried to sing for us – in German. He sang off-key and with tears streaming down his face.

"This is better than Africa", he said, as he polished off the Aloxe-Corton. "I thought we'd die of thirst. Why we brought the dog along, I don't know. Once I suggested that we kill him and eat him – he was only a handful. Fortunately he ran away and got lost in the desert." He stopped and made a wry grimace. "I've eaten worse than dogs, you know. I've eaten rats and snakes ... You can eat anything if you're hungry enough. You Americans don't know what it is to starve ... "

"We don't eh?" I gave Mona a look.

"We've starved all right", she said.

"You starved in the midst of plenty", said Carl. "There *was* food around, only you couldn't afford it. That's different. Here everybody starved ... and plenty. I was starving too, like every one else. I starved in Austria, in Germany, in Czechoslovakia, in Hungary, in Romania, in France, in Italy. But we're not starving now, are we? We're not going to starve ever again, are we? Not until the next war anyway."

Talking about his starving days he grew merrier and merrier. Suddenly an old woman came up to us and asked if she might have a crust of bread. Mona immediately fixed her a healthy looking sandwich and invited her to sit down.

"You shouldn't do that", said Carl. "You embarrass her." With that he offered her the bottle, what was left of it – it was only the second one – and urged her to drink. "Watch, she'll ask me for a cigarette in a moment. Then we'll pack her off."

Mona meanwhile was going through her
purse in search of loose change.

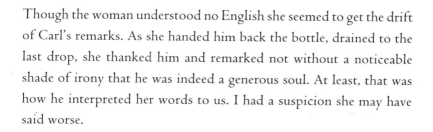

"Don't do that", said
Carl, "She's got
plenty. If I had what
she's got hidden
away in her stock-
ing I'd feel rich.
Don't be too sym-
pathetic. There are
millions of them
around. You didn't come
here to solve the social
problem."

Though the woman understood no English she seemed to get the drift
of Carl's remarks. As she handed him back the bottle, drained to the
last drop, she thanked him and remarked not without a noticeable
shade of irony that he was indeed a generous soul. At least, that was
how he interpreted her words to us. I had a suspicion she may have
said worse.

"The trouble with you people is", he went on after the old woman had
left, "you don't know how to give. There's an art to giving, just as there
is to begging. I don't know how to beg, unfortunately, but I know how
to give. You seem to think that money solves everything. She might
have felt better, you know, if you had just given her the crust of bread
she asked for. The French don't like to be treated like beggars, even
when they beg. They're proud. But she was a professional. What she
wanted was the wine, not the food. She could hardly get the food
down, didn't you notice? And then handing her all that change ... she
just thought you were crazy. You *are* crazy too. If I hadn't spoken you

might have given her fifty francs. Give it to *me*, if you must throw your money away. I can put it to good use. I could get my typewriter out of hock, for one thing. And retrieve my laundry. I haven't put a clean shirt on for two weeks now."

"How did you manage to buy the wine?" I put in.

He blushed. "Don't ask me", he said.

So the day began. After a while, after we had taken a snooze on the grass, we got up and strolled about. Our steps led us in the direction of Notre Dame. We had to steer through that squalid section off the Place St. Michel — the rue St. Severin, the rue de la Huchette, and so on. A fascinating world, I thought, never dreaming that it would one day be associated with the publication of my books. In front of Notre Dame we debated whether to climb the winding stairs to the level of the gargoyles or not.

"Some other time", said Carl. "Anybody can go to see Notre Dame. I've never been in it, to tell you the truth, and I don't intend to see it now. I'm sick of cathedrals and museums and art galleries. Let's sit down somewhere and have a coffee."

"Let's go to Ste. Chapelle at least", said Mona, as we sipped our coffee.

"Don't you want something with your coffee?" said Carl, ignoring her suggestion. He called the waiter over and ordered a cognac for himself. "You'll have Chartreuse, I suppose?" He looked at Mona as if to say — I know your vices.

"You don't want to go to Ste. Chapelle", he said. "You should go early in the morning, when you have a bad hangover. That's the only time to appreciate real beauty. Now we're digesting our food. We ate too much."

"You mean drank too much", said Mona.

"Anyway you like", said Carl. "Only it's not the time for visiting cathedrals. Or the Flea Market. If it wasn't so early I'd take you to a bordel. I could do with a good lay now. It doesn't cost very much either. Maybe we ought to have a look at the St. Denis quarter. You haven't seen any real whores yet, I'll bet. The best ones are those with a few teeth missing. I like them on the ugly side. It's a change from the American beauty type. You must get tired of see-

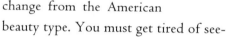

ing nothing but beautiful women. Just the same, I wish my Eileen were here now. I could give her a good lay, even though she is a beauty."

Evening found us having an aperitif at the Café Wepler, in Mont-mar-tre. We were weary and a bit groggy now. The *terrasse* was sprinkled with whores, some of them very attractive, I thought.

Joey", he said, "I'm going to call you Joe from now on. Val doesn't suit you at all. It sounds sissified. Let *her* call you that, if she likes. Anyway, what I want to say is — have you enough money on you to afford a good meal?"

"Ask Mona", I said. "She handles the exchequer."

He turned to Mona. "How about it, cutie? How many thousand francs have you left?"

"Where *is* your restaurant?" Mona parried, rather cagily I thought.

"Not very far. But we'll have to take a cab ... First let's have another drink." He called the waiter. "Three Pernods!" he commanded.

It was another half-hour before we rose to our feet. To my surprise I felt myself swaying.

"You're drunk", said Mona.

"That's fine", said Carl. "The hors d'oeuvre will settle his stomach."

"Couldn't we walk a ways first?"

"That'll only make it worse", said Carl. "He's had enough walking already; he needs food. Good food. A pheasant or a capon, or a juicy chateaubriand. I know exactly the place. But it's going to cost you something, I warn you."

"Don't worry", said Mona. "Only don't take us to the Crillon."

"You've got some American Express checks on you, I hope?" said Carl. "Americans always carry Express cheeks, I notice."

The restaurant was somewhere near the Bourse, it seemed to me. It was small, cosy, intimate – and expensive. Every dish was about three times the price of what we were accustomed to pay for an entire meal. The wines were also expensive, but the best. He certainly had taste, this rascal Carl. As if to explain himself he informed us that he only ate here about once a year, and always as someone's guest, naturally.

As I glanced around the room it seemed to me that most of the clientele was composed of eminent individuals. Some of the older men resembled famous writers or painters. One was a ringer for Anatole France; another might have passed for Joris Karl Huysmans. The women were all exquisitely gowned and exceedingly attractive, even the older ones. It seemed to me that they regarded us as intruders.

We were in high spirits and our tongues were wagging. I realized that we were the only ones talking English and that we were talking rather loudly. But I had no idea how offensive our voices sounded until an elderly and distinguished looking gentleman came over from a corner of the room and, addressing Carl, who was the chief offender — or perhaps looked more like a European — requested us in a polite but nevertheless insulting manner to please moderate our tone. He spoke in French, of course, and when Carl, who was blushing like a pig, replied in perfect French, he seemed taken aback. After excusing himself for having delivered such an admonition he said: "But why don't you speak French together? English is rather grating on the ear, you must admit." Whereupon Carl informed him that we were Americans, newly arrived, and knew only a few words of French.

"But you, Monsieur, you are not French, yet you speak the language fluently, and with scarcely a trace of accent."

To which Carl replied that his mother was French, but that he had been raised in Budapest, which accounted for his accent. Then he added, with a malicious twinkle in his eye, that he had learned his English in the insane asylum.

That finished the conversation. "I see", said the man, and turned on his heel.

Under his breath Carl promptly informed us that the old geezer was a genuine prick. "Did you notice that he was wearing the Legion of Honor? That's bad in itself. He's probably a retired coal merchant. Anyone can get the Legion of Honor today; no one with sense wears the damned thing."

Suddenly I realized that we had taken to whispering, or so it seemed. "What are we whispering for?" I asked.

"Yeah", said Carl, raising his voice a little, "fuck this place! I'm never coming here again. He insulted us, do you realize that? Maybe he took us for Huns." He looked me in the eye and added: "You could pass for a German, do you know that?"

"But never for an Austrian, eh? Or a Hungarian?"

"That's right, Joey, you're catching on."

"Why don't we go to Vienna?" said Mona suddenly.

"Don't!" said Carl. "Go to Klagenfurt or some other god forsaken place."

"What about Budapest?"

"That's not so bad, especially if you don't speak the language. I starved there too, remember? I like the Hungarian women, but not the men. Why don't you go to Syracuse or Fez or Constantinople? You've got money to burn. Spend it! See the world. Go to India or China or Siam. I'll bet you never thought of Siam."

"We're not as rich as you imagine", said Mona. "If we eat like this very often we'll be broke in a month."

"As long as you've got American Express checks you're okay", said Carl. "Have you any on you now? I'd like to look at one again. Eileen always had a wad of them."

"You should find another Eileen", I
put in.

"I've got a Czech cunt now",
said Carl. "She's not so hot to
look at but she's a good lay.
Only she doesn't have any
money. Now and then I have
to buy her a meal."

"What became of Irma, the
German girl?" asked Mona.

He made a strange grimace and
downed the rest of his wine before
replying. "She turned Lesbian on
me", he said. From his expression one
would think it was the most humiliating thing
that could have happened to him.

I was about to say something when he continued. "She's still good for
a lay occasionally, but it's not the same anymore. She doesn't put her
heart in it."

"Is she still around?" asked Mona.

"Sure", said Carl. "You can find her at Dominique's any evening. She
likes the food there."

"I thought she was an interesting person", said Mona. "Stasia liked
her too."

"Stasia is an angel", said Carl. "Irma's just an intellectual bitch. If you
don't find her at Dominique's you can find her later in the evening at
Le Monocle."

"Oh?" said Mona. "Is that still going? I thought it had been closed by the police.

"It was ... for a time. But there are so many Germans and Scandinavians here now they had to let them open it again. I hate the place. I'd rather go to the Bal Negre."

"What about the Bal Tabarin?" said Mona.

"That's for tourists ... like you", said Carl.

"Oh, tell Val about the Grand Guignol, won't you?"

"It's no good", said Carl promptly. "Let *me* show him where to go. *You* can go to the Folies Bergère, if you like."

"I want to go home", I said. "Back to the hotel. I'm beginning to feel woozy."

When we hit the street Carl took my arm and said: "You know, Joey, I think that man who insulted us was Jules Romains, I suppose you never heard of him. He's a bore, take it from me. He's written only one book I like. That's *The Death of a Nobody*. It's humorous. Read it some time. It must be translated by this time."

"Don't you read any German writers anymore?" I asked.

"There aren't any good German writers anymore", he replied. "Unless you call Wassermann a German writer."

"Well, isn't he? I know Wassermann's work. I like him too. What is he, if he isn't a German?"

"He's a German Jew", said Carl. "That's why you like him. In a way he's closer to the Russians than the Germans."

"Precisely", I said. "But he's a German writer, just the same. Just as Proust is a French writer, although he's half Jewish."

"No French writer has ever written like
Proust, Joey. All these people of
mixed blood contribute something
new and strange to the language.
Sometimes they're more German
than the Germans, or more
French than the French. Take
your Lafcadio Hearn, for instance. He was a strange mixture, but his English is of the
best. Or take Conrad. His is a very
special kind of English, but it's
English, isn't it? Would you call *him*
an English writer?"

I didn't bother to answer. I was too full of wine
and food. "I'll answer you another time", I said. "Let's hop this cab,
what do you say?"

HENRY MILLER

PARIS

HENRY + MONA

Part Three

One afternoon a few days later, as we were about to take a seat at the Dôme, who pops up but MacGregor.

"*Henry*, you bastard, where have you been? I've been looking all over Paris for you. Sit down, sit down! Let's drink to the occasion."

"Excuse me, Val", said Mona, "I'll be back in a little while. Irma is waiting for me across the street."

"Who's Irma?" said MacGregor, obviously annoyed.

"Nobody", I said. "Forget it."

"I don't think she likes me. What's she got against me anyway?"

"Forget it", I said. "How are you anyway? When did you get here? And where's Guelda?"

He gave me a broad grin. "Take it easy", he said. "It's a long story."

Just then a young American appeared and took a seat beside us. "My cousin", said MacGregor. "You don't remember him, I suppose. Tillotson's his name. Just call him Bruce."

We shook hands and once again I inquired about Guelda.

"Where is she?" asked MacGregor.

"Up in the room, sleeping it off", young Bruce replied.

"What a night! " said MacGregor. "You know the Hôtel des Ecoles, don't you? Right around the corner. I thought they would put us out this morning. Everybody drunk and yelling and singing." He turned to Bruce. "What happened to that Negress you brought home? You know where we were, Hen? At the Bal Negre. What a joint! 'We've got to go there some night – without the women. Wait a minute. Why the hell didn't you look me up when you got here? I told you you could leave word for me at the American Express. Well, anyway, you're here. Now we can see Paris together. A great place, eh? Did you get your end in yet? I suppose you've been to Montmartre, the Moulin Rouge and all that? No? What are you doing with yourself?"

"Tell me about Guelda", I said. "Did it go off like you planned?"

He leaned back and chuckled softly, "Ask Bruce", he said.

"I want to hear it from *you*."

"It's a long story, Hen. Have you got time to listen?"

"All the time in the world", I replied.

He went into it in detail, how he got a cabin next to hers, how he waited till morning to catch her on deck and surprise her ... the whole business from A to Izzit.

"How did she take it? Was she happy?"

"Of course she was", he replied, "only she pretended not to show it at first. But after the champagne, the flowers and all that she warmed up. But she wouldn't go to bed with me. I had to wait till the other night – can you imagine – when I got her good and soused."

"How does she like Paris?"

"She's crazy about it. Now she
wants to see the Chateau country, I
should hire a car and all that. We
may go tomorrow. Will you be
here when we get back? I want to
marry her here in Paris, if I can.
And you're goin' to be best
man."

"Don't rush her", I said. "Remember, she likes to be coaxed."

"I know how to handle her, Hen.
Now that I'm layin' her I can get her to do
anything. She was a virgin, you know. Made quite a fuss about it too.
You know how these Catholics are. Anyway, she likes it. I can't give
her enough, to tell you the truth."

"She didn't like what happened last night too much", Bruce inter-
jected.

"Sure, I know", said MacGregor. "But you can't blame her. It was all
your fault, goddamn it. Bringing that colored girl along and that other
couple you picked up somewhere. Who were they anyhow?"

"Search me", said Bruce. "I never saw them before."

"What do you mean?" I said. "All six of you fucking in the same
room?"

Bruce began to snicker.

"What he means, Hen, is that I was so drunk I tried to make the colored girl too. Naturally Guelda got miffed. I had a job explaining that one."

"You don't think she'll run off and leave you?" I said.

"Who, Guelda? Not on your life. *We're in love.* She'll be O.K. when she wakes up. It's Paris, what the hell. I keep telling her that all the time. She's got to relax. Besides, if she wants to go to confession, there's a hundred churches to choose from. It's the Scotch in her that makes her queasy."

"So you're going to the Chateau country."

"Yeah, what about coming with us? If that wife of yours ... what's her name again?"

"Mona."

"Yeah, Mona. if she doesn't want to come along, *you* come. I promise you a good time. You've got some money now, I suppose."

"Plenty", I replied.

He shook his head. "That's the first time I ever heard you say that. What did you do ... rob a bank?"

I grinned.

"Okay. Don't tell me. I know you never got it honestly."

Bruce wanted another round of drinks. He beckoned to the garçon but the latter appeared to take no notice. Then he clapped his hands, and when that failed he put two fingers in his mouth and whistled.

"Stupid bastards", he muttered. "Never around when you want'em."

The garçon finally came. He
ordered in French, good
French, to my surprise. When
I inquired where he had
picked up the language he
replied "in High School.
Nothing to it", he added.
"It's easy."

When I asked him what
he thought of France and
of the French, he answered:
"Much like any other place".
He didn't think much of the
French as a people. Too
independent.

And rather shabby.

Had he talked to any of them? A few, yes. In bars mostly.

"And you didn't find them exciting?"

"What's exciting about them?" he replied. "They're just like any other
people, far as I can see."

"What other people do you know?" I asked.

"Don't listen to him " said MacGregor. "He's just a spoiled brat. I
don't know why the hell I took him along with me."

"I know why", said Bruce. "Because I can talk French. You should hear
him trying to order a ham sandwich."

"Listen, Hen, where are you staying? I want to see you soon as I set
back."

I gave him a false address, on the rue Madame.

"What do you know", he said. "Ain't that where Gertrude Stein lives?"

"I don't know", I said.

"It's the rue de Fleurus", said Bruce.

"What's the difference?" said MacGregor. "We're not interested in *her*. By the way, Hen, have you run into Hemingway yet? I hear he hangs out at the Jockey Club."

"You're wrong", said Bruce. "He hangs out at the Deux Magots ... or Jimmy's Bar."

"How do you know so damned much?" said MacGregor. "I suppose you can tell us where to meet Picasso too."

"Sure I can", said Bruce. "That's easy. Ask me a hard one."

"All right", said MacGregor. "Where do I find Utrillo?"

That seemed to stump him. "He's dead, I think", he replied.

"He's not neither", said MacGregor. "Besides, you don't know who I'm talking about. I'll ask you another, since you're so fuckin' smart. Where does Francis Carco hang out? Answer me that!"

"Never heard of him", said Bruce.

"There you are", said MacGregor. "He knows everybody except the most colorful figure in all Montmartre."

"And how do you know about him?" I put in.

"I read about him", said MacGregor. "That's how."

"By the way", he added, "That wife of yours hasn't turned up yet. Does she know her way around?"

"Don't worry about *her*", I replied. "She's probably sitting
with André Gide or Hans
Arp."

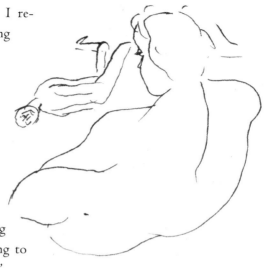

"Or Gertrude Stein",
chirped MacGregor.
"She's a strange gal,
Henry. You don't mind
my saying so? What was
she doing here on her own
last year? Just touring
Europe? What are you going to
do ... stay in Paris or what?"

"I think we'll travel."

"Like where?"

"Austria, Hungary, Germany, Italy ..."

"You must really be in the money. Or are you hitch-hiking?"

"We travel first class only."

"I'll remember that", said MacGregor, "in case I go broke".

"Good", I said. "See me any time. I can always let you have a hundred
or two, maybe more. Look me up when you get back; maybe we can
have dinner together at Maxim's."

"Why not make it the Ritz ... or the Crillon?"

"Listen, I've got to go now. Got to find Mona." I started to shake
hands.

"What about paying for the drinks?"

"Certainly", I said. "With pleasure. I thought you had invited *me* to sit down."

"Run along", he said. "I was just trying you out, you bastard."

"Say hello to Guelda for me", I shouted, as I made off.

It took me a half hour or more to find Mona and her friend Irma. Finally I caught sight of them seated on the *terrasse* of the Closerie des Lilas. They didn't seem to be too delighted to see me. Apparently they were in the midst of a discussion about German authors. Irma had just been talking about Fritz von Unruh, of all people. She was from Marienbad, Irma, but had lived all over Germany. Her English was excellent and her French too. I could see what Carl meant when he referred to her as an intellectual bitch. Nevertheless there was something attractive about her; I couldn't detect the Lesbian in her immediately. It was Mona, as usual, who seemed to be making the advances.

As Irma rattled on about Fritz von Unruh, Hugo von Hoffmansthal, Wedekind, Werfel et alia, I was amazed to observe how much Mona seemed to know about these authors. It was true, of course, that she had had parts in a number of German plays when they were given at the Theatre Guild, but aside from the playwrights, aside from Wassermann whom everybody was reading at the time, aside from Thomas Mann and Rilke whose names were bywords, I had never heard her dwell on German literature. When I expressed my amazement she informed me that I must have forgotten our midnight conversations after the theatre. She even reminded me of the discussions she used to hold with her father, which she had related in detail time and again. To top it all she reminded me of our evenings with Ulric, when I read aloud to him from Gottfried Benn, Kurt Shwitters and such like. And what about Heinrich Mann — had I forgotten my enthusiasm for him?

The conversation began to sparkle. Irma seemed delighted that I had at least an inkling of contemporary German literature. She was trying to write herself, poetry principally, and had just begun a novel, her first. She recited a few poems of Rilke's, then something of her own — all in German, of course — while Mona shook her head approvingly and ordered more drinks. At this point Irma suddenly inquired if she might not see some of Mona's work. I wondered what the answer would be.

"I've given up writing", Mona answered. "One writer in the family is enough", and she looked at me.

Evidently Irma didn't know that I was a writer. She reacted as if it were the last thing on earth she expected to hear.

"What did you think he was?" asked Mona.

Irma squirmed a bit, then blurted out: "I thought he might be a dentist or a surgeon".

I laughed. "I almost became a clergyman", I said.

"That doesn't surprise me at all", said Irma. "With the proper attire you could easily pass for a pastor."

69

"Nonsense!" Mona exclaimed. "He may be serious, perhaps too serious at times, but a minister of the gospel ... *never!* You should see what he writes, that would disabuse you quickly."

"What *do* you write, if I may ask?" said Irma.

"Ask Mona", I replied. "She knows better than I."

"I'll show you his work sometime", said Mona by way of answer.

Assuming that I was somebody in the world of American letters, Irma now suggested that we meet some of her friends, all poets, playwrights, actors, dancers.

"Where?" I said. "At the Monocle?"

"The Monocle?" She opened wide her eyes. "Why the Monocle?"

"I thought that was your hang-out", I replied.

"Whatever gave you that idea? I loathe the place."

Said Mona: "It was Carl who told him that."

"I thought so", said Irma. "That's his way of getting even with me. He tries to pretend I've turned Lesbian."

"What's wrong with being a Lesbian?"

She hesitated a moment. "Nothing, really. Only I'm not one. Right now I'm pregnant, if that means anything to you."

I didn't know what to say to this. I waited to see if she would embroider on it.

Mona now spoke up. "You don't mind, Val, do you, if I walk Irma back to her room? She wants to show me something. I'll be home soon."

"Of course not", I said, knowing damned
well that Irma had nothing to show
unless it was a pair of beautiful
teats.

I rose to go.

"Why don't you
have dinner with
your friend
MacGregor?" said
Mona. "How is he, by
the way?"

"Just fine", I said. I started
off. "See you later."

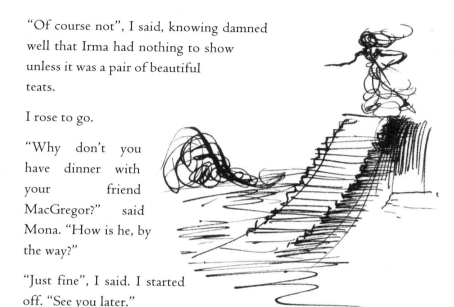

Suddenly I heard her running after me. I turned round.

"Val, I'll be home in just a little while. Wait for me. You're not
worried about Irma, are you?"

"Why should I be? She seems like a nice girl."

"She's in trouble, Val. That's why I want to talk to her ... alone."

"Okay. Don't worry about me. I'll have a little look around meanwhile. So long now."

I watched her run back to the table. As she sat down Irma waved
goodbye to me.

"A Lesbian and pregnant", I mumbled to myself. "What a pickle!"
And as I sauntered off I began thinking of Berlin, the Berlin of after
the war, with its cabarets, its dives, its homosexual atmosphere, its
misery, starvation, despair and hopelessness. And there was Irma, in

my mind, sitting at a table in a smoke-filled joint, a telephone at her elbow, and a long, thin cigar in her mouth. Why not? She was just the type. Attractive, open-minded. intelligent, desperate. There were thousands like her. The miracle was that any of them had survived. Irma would always manage to survive. She would survive even if it were only on Rilke – or Fritz von Unruh. She could be a mannikin today, an actress tomorrow, and a drug vendor the day after. She knew how to drift with the tide. And, if my guess was right, she would be richer by fifty or a hundred dollars by the time Mona left her.

By the time another two or three weeks had passed I was getting fed up with Paris. Every day we seemed to pick up another acquaintance, usually some starving poet or painter. We never did get to see Reichel's paintings and I never did meet any of those fabulous artists such as Kokoschka, Marcel Duchamp, Vlaminck, Utrillo. Once I caught a glimpse of Edgar Varese standing in the doorway of the Dôme. "Let me introduce you", said Mona, but I was too shy. I found more enjoyment just meandering through the streets, studying the titles of books in the shop windows, peering into art galleries, or gazing at the marvellous vegetables, meats, fruit and other edibles which seemed to literally engulf one in certain busy sections of the city. Of course we went to Les Halles and the Jardin du Palais Royal, to the Louvre, the Cluny Museum (chiefly to see the chastity belts),

to the Mosque and the Jardin des Plan-
tes. But we never got to the Bal
Negre nor the Monocle nor to
any of the celebrated bor-
dels. A good part of the
time, it seemed to me, was
spent sitting in cafés and
restaurants, talking to
people who bored me to
tears. We went once to the
Folies Bergère, which I
found excruciatingly dull, but
never to the Moulin Rouge.
When I found a quarter which I
thought highly interesting, such as the Jewish quarter in the St. Paul
district, Mona was utterly apathetic. I needed a male companion to
explore the city with me, and I had found none. I met Carl several
times, but he too preferred to sit on his ass somewhere and chew the
fat.

One day, while having a drink with Borowski, he asked why we didn't
get out and see the country. Why not get bicycles, for instance, and
head for the Midi? There was so much to see, why waste time in Paris?
He took a paper napkin and outlined a route itinerary for us. It all
sounded intriguing and very simple. Mona had never ridden a bicycle,
but was willing to learn.

A few days later we went to a shop near the Porte Maillot and picked
out two sturdy bikes. Since she didn't know how to ride we had to
walk back to the hotel, pushing the bikes. It was a long walk back to
the rue Bonaparte and we were stared at all the way. Just as we came
within a block of the hotel suddenly I felt a tremendous whack over
the shoulder and before I could turn around the lunatic who had

struck me began smashing the tires and the spokes with a big stick. I caught him by the shoulders and pushed him against the wall, only it so happened that what I took for a wall was a door which swung open, our assailant fell head backwards and lay there moaning. Immediately a crowd gathered, all expressing sympathy for the poor old man who had been knocked down by this brute of an American. I looked around helplessly, trying to explain, in English, that it was not my fault, that the old duffer was crazy and so on, but no one seemed to understand me, nor did any one make an effort to understand. Fortunately the garçon of our hotel suddenly appeared and rescued us. The bikes had to be taken to a repair shop, of course.

A day or two later I began giving Mona lessons on the rue Visconti. It was no go. Once again the garçon came to our rescue. He agreed to give her instructions a half-hour each day. Always on the rue Visconti.

I knew she would never be able to make it through the Paris traffic, so I suggested that we take the train as far as Fontainebleau and there begin our cycling trip.

What a pity that I knew nothing then of that mysterious figure Gurdjiev who was living then in Fontainebleau. Or of Milosz, the Lithuanian poet, who was also living there. Never did I dream that twenty-five years later I would be sitting in La Guilde du Livre in Lausanne waiting to know if I could obtain a copy of his little book called *The Key to the Apocalypse.*

In Fontainebleau Mona had a few days of practice, enough to give her confidence to begin the journey. Borowski had told us that we would find it easier following the canals, which I decided to do. I forgot that the tow paths were narrow and that Mona was still jittery. Several times she narrowly missed tumbling into the canal.

Finally we arrived at the little town of Auxerre on
the river Yonne. That
was our first wonder-
ful halting place. It
must have been late
afternoon when we
pulled up at a little
café and ordered
drinks. I remember
the cathedral in the
distance, the peace
and serenity which
emanated from the
place. Suddenly I realized
that we were in France, that it

was another completely different world from Paris. I felt so good I
could have remained in that spot forever. After we had found a hotel
for the night we went in search of a restaurant. The food seemed
infinitely better than what we had had in Paris. The vin ordinaire was
better also. And the owners of the restaurant were most congenial,
delighted, it seemed, to have two Americans as their guests. They even
tried to speak a little English, and when they learned that we hailed
from New York, they looked at us as if we were bold adventurers.
That night the church bells rang out with new meaning. All was peace
and joy. It was the France I had so often dreamed of, and for once the
reality was better than the dream.

Leisurely we made our way to Dijon. At midday we usually bought
ourselves bread, salami, cheese, olives and a bottle of wine, which we
ate by the roadside under a shady tree. It made no difference whether
we made ten miles or thirty each day. Time meant nothing. We had
American Express checks in our pockets and. four stout legs to carry

us along. The weather remained ideal, the roads were uncluttered, the world lay before us.

We arrived in Dijon around noon one day, took a seat at a café and soon found ourselves surrounded by a group of students who eyed us curiously. Finally one of them came over to our table and, addressing us in English, asked if we were from England. We asked him to sit down and have a drink with us. He was from Germany, it turned out, and very eager to talk to us, particularly when he learned that we were not English but American.

Though he couldn't keep his eyes off Mona I noticed that he was also trying to size me up. My costume — tweed coat and knickerbockers — intrigued him no end. Finally he summoned the courage to ask me if I was by chance a clergyman, perhaps a Presbyterian minister.

"Why?" said Mona. "What's wrong with him?"

"Oh, there's nothing wrong", he answered. "He just has the look of a pastor."

I didn't know whether to be amused or annoyed.

"Maybe you can tell us where to find a modest hotel", I said.

Indeed he could. He would escort us to one immediately, with pleasure. We finished our drinks and went along with him. Since he had been so kind we invited him to have lunch with us. His eyes glistened at this. Obviously he didn't eat regularly every day.

Over the coffee and liqueurs he began to unburden himself. The long and short of it was that he owed two months' back room rent and hadn't a cent to live on. He confessed that he had thrust himself upon us in the hope of getting aid. We must forgive him, he said, because he was absolutely desperate. We told him we understood, that we were often in the same plight ourselves — which he didn't believe, of course

— and thereupon handed him one of
our Express checks. He blushed to
the roots of his hair, thanked us
profusely, and asked if there
was anything more he could
do for us, anything at all, it
would make him happy.
Adding — the old refrain —
that Americans were the
most generous souls on
earth.

Suddenly he said: "If
you are not a minister of
the gospel, sir, may I ask
what it is you do? Are you a physician
perhaps?"

"I'm a writer", I replied. "A writer of no importance. I haven't yet sold
a story or an article to any editor. We live by our wits ... do you know
what that means? We've been hungry for days on end, we've robbed
our friends, we've cheated the tradespeople, we've lived a dog's life
ever since I decided to be a writer. Don't ask me how we got here —
it's too long a story. You think you're poor. We have thousands in
America who would love to be in your position. You haven't tasted
anything yet. You were probably too young to go to war and you'll be
too old for the next war, let's hope. Americans are generous, not out
of good will but because life is too easy. That is, for those who have
the money. The rest of us don't count. Today we have American
Express checks. Tomorrow we may be begging for help, just like you.
Today nobody wants my work; tomorrow I may be on the way to
becoming a millionaire. But don't go to America if you can make an
honest living elsewhere... I think we'll leave you now. It's time for a

nap. The point is to take it nice and easy — if you can. Good luck to you! *Auf wiederseh'n!*

Since it was rich in history we made a survey of the town, absorbing what we could of its Burgundian flavor. I wasn't too impressed, I must confess, even though, as Mona reminded me, Edgar Varese was a Burgundian. (Years later, in New York, I was to discover for myself what a marvellous Burgundian he is.) We had a stupendous dinner in a celebrated restaurant over a marvellous bottle of Beaune. They knew how to eat, the Burgundians. But it struck me as a dopey, sleepy, mournful town, despite the good food and the good wines.

Now and then we stopped off to admire a cathedral or a fortress or some desolate castle. I remember Vezelay in particular; Borowski had recommended seeing the Romanesque church there. It was market day when we made our way to the Square. Our costume always seemed to arouse attention. As we moved about from one stall to another we were gently pelted with edibles by the country gawks who stared and giggled at us unashamedly.

Now and then, when Mona was weary, we would hop a train for a few miles. Somewhere before or after Lyon — could it have been La Voulte, I wonder? — while seated at a café in a turn of the road I had one of those hallucinatory visitations which left me high and dry for hours to come. Somehow, why I could never understand, I had the feeling that I had sat in this same spot some time in the past, a past so distant that it could only have been in another incarnation. Years later, on a solo bike trip through this same region, I tried desperately to locate this spot, but without success. Coming out of the trance I remember distinctly speculating as to whether I had read Ruskin's *Bible of Amiens* or not. It seemed desperately important, at the moment, to visit the cathedral of Amiens. Ruskin, Ruskin! Was it Ruskin who wrote that book? Or was it Proust? Anyway, though I had

never seen the cathedral, suddenly it stood before me as clear as could be, so touchingly real and tangible that I was on the point of tears.

How we ever got through Lyon without an accident I don't know. It's a city that has never had any appeal for me, although the panorama from above is exciting. We had decided to stop off for the night in Vienne, ancient capital of Southern Gaul. Vienne I fell in love with immediately. Once again a strange thing occurred. It was night and we had left the hotel for a short stroll. Suddenly I espied a café with a huge billiard table in the center of it and above the table a swinging lamp. It was almost a replica of the painting by Van Gogh. We entered and watched the Annamite soldiers knock the balls around. I was so bewitched I couldn't make the effort to sit down at a table and order coffee. We just stood there near the entrance and gaped. Once again I revisited the town — years later — and walked my legs off trying to find this café. But again no luck. It had vanished like a dream. Nor could I find a single Annamite soldier.

The next town which made an impression on me was Orange. It remains in my memory in a sort of picture postcard  way. It was terribly hot, dusty, empty of people. I remember the way the awning flapped listlessly as we took our seats outside. The arch was there, as it had been for many a century, but it was a detached arch, having nothing to do with the Romans who had built it. It was there like an object *déjà vu.* Some years later — once again — I am watching a film of Jean Gabin's and strike me dead if it isn't the very same café that he walks into, the same listless awning, the same zinc bar.

Soon came Avignon and Tarascon, charming places, I thought, just made for a writer or a letter carrier. Why not settle down here? Settle for a thousand year sleep in the womb of antiquity. So drowsy, so out of the running, so unconcerned with the problems of the world. The spirit of the Midi was at last beginning to make itself felt. To be lazy, to bask in the sun, to waddle about in pantoufles, to talk nonsense with one's neighbor, to sit by a stream with hook and line and dream of yesterday. To get nowhere passionately. To munch olives, sip a Pernod, bite into a salami. In Paris they were running around like ants. Literary commotion. Politics. Who's going to win the Prix Femina or the Prix Goncourt? What do you think of Jules Romains or some other blunderbuss? Have you any money on you? A barbarous people, the Parisians. Foreigners. No question about it. Here in the Midi nobody gets published, unless a miracle occurs. Everyone is an artist, even if he is only a butcher. Here there is talk. Everyone is descended from some great poet, troubador or Minnesinger. Here one can lie with impunity. They are not lies, but tabulations. Here exaggeration is the norm. Nobody is interested in facts. Facts are dead, like the horse in the gutter. Naturally the sewage is archaic. It was better in Roman times. One sits amidst the ruins of history and twiddles his thumbs. What could be better?

And not far away lies Les Baux — or rather stands erect on gigantic rock stilts. Formidable place, as if torn from some forgotten planet. The Baux family — cruel, fiendish buggers, if one is to believe the record. (How come Gilles de Rais never settled here?) And to think that not too far away, in a slightly different direction, lies the utterly romantic village of Vaucluse [sic]. Something monstrous about Les Baux; something staggering to the eye. Reminiscent of Arizona and Nevada, only Les Baux has a history, a bloody, horrible one at that.

Well, on to Arles, where civilization again raises its head, where all is man-sized and teeming with memories. To think that once it was a sea port, more important by far than Marseilles. And now almost as dead as Bruges, where too the waters once lapped the stone walls.

In Arles there were posters everywhere announcing the coming bull-fight in Nimes; we decided to go, neither of us having seen a bullfight before. In the train we fell into conversation with two young French-men who lived in Arles. They spoke English fairly well and, as we soon discovered, were *aficionados*. One was called Georges, the other Paul, comrades from college days. After the bullfight we went back to Arles and had dinner together. They were wonderful companions, jolly, well read, eager to do anything that would please us. We stayed on a few days, visiting their friends and making excursions into the country-side. When it came time to part they actually had tears in their eyes. We told them we were going on to Marseilles, Nice, Monte Carlo.

They gave us their cards and said they might meet us in Nice, as they were due to go there soon. We promised to keep in touch with one another.

Coming down a steep hill leading into Marseilles, Mona's bike got out of control and before I could stop her, her front wheel got caught in the trolley tracks and she took a bad spill. One leg was badly cut up. We took a room nearby and there she lay abed for almost two weeks. I decided that we had had enough of bike riding and sold the wheels for a song. When she was able to move we took the train to Monte Carlo, stayed there a few days, then went back to Nice. We were running short of cash by now and had to send our bank book to New York where we had money in a savings account. We thought it would only be a matter of days before we received our money, but it turned out otherwise.

Finally we were down to our last cent. We decided to write Paul and Georges and tell them of our predicament. Walking along the Promenade des Anglais the next day, hungry as wolves since we had eaten nothing since lunch the day before, we came to a bootblack stand owned by a big burly Negro. We nodded instinctively and with that the fellow advanced a few steps and asked if I didn't want my shoes shined. He had a deep, booming voice with a Georgia accent. Something inside me said "Go ahead, deliver it!"

In a moment I explained to him that more important than a shine was a good meal, that we hadn't eaten for forty-eight hours.

"Where you all from?" he asked with a big, kindly smile.

"New York", I replied.

He put out his hand, first to me, then to Mona, and said: "I've been there too, brother. What's the trouble?"

I explained quickly that we were
waiting for money to come
from our bank in New
York.

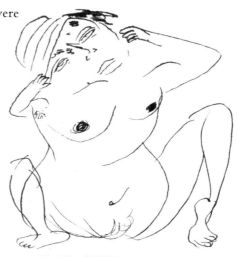

"Have you got a place
to stay?" he asked.

We gave him the name
of the hotel we were
staying at and explained
that we expected our
French friends to show up
any day.

"Don't let it worry you", he said promptly. And with that he fished
out some francs and handed them to us. Then added: "Come here
every day around this time and I'll see that you get enough to eat.
We're Americans, ain't we?" Then he informed us where we could eat
cheaply and well.

Mona was in tears as we shook hands and toddled off to in search of
the restaurant he had suggested.

"You know something?" I said. "I wonder what he would have
thought if he knew that we gave our last twenty bucks to a Gypsy
violinist."

"It was your fault", she said. "You shouldn't have asked him to play
for you. They're thieves, you know that."

"Sure", I said, "I know that. But how was I to know that you'd be
foolish enough to give him twenty bucks? Five would have been
plenty."

"One doesn't stop to count", she replied, "in a moment like that."

"He is a peach of a guy, that Nigger", I said.

"Don't say Nigger, Val."

"I don't mean any harm by it. What do you want to do, make a gentleman of him?"

"A prince, you mean. He's a real prince. Catch a white man doing that for us!"

When we got back to the hotel there was a telegram for us from Georges and Paul. They were arriving the next day.

"I guess we're fixed", I said.

"Don't be too sure", said Mona. "They don't strike me as being rich."

Presently she had an idea. "If they can lend us just a little money, Val", she said, "I'll wire Borowski — he'll certainly help us out."

The next morning our friends showed up at the hotel, their faces beaming. They didn't have much money, they quickly informed us, but they would speak to the proprietor of the hotel, make sure he didn't turn us out, and perhaps get him to give us dinner on credit. They handed us some francs apologetically and assured us that we had nothing to worry about. We in turn assured them that our money would turn up any day. We then went to the Post Office where Mona got off a telegram to Borowski.

"How much did you ask for?" I inquired as soon as we were alone.

"A hundred dollars."

"Do you think he can spare that much?"

"Of course", she replied. "He's not poor, Borowski."

A few hours later there came his reply.
"Sorry, but I don't have that much
money to spare. Letter following."

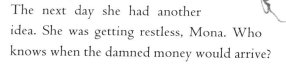

"I'd never have believed
it", she said, crumpling
the telegram in her hand.

"Guess we've got to rely
on that Prince of a
Nigger", said I. "Any-
how, we're sure of three
meals a day for a while."

The next day she had another
idea. She was getting restless, Mona. Who
knows when the damned money would arrive?

"I tell you what we'll do", she confided. "We'll go to the American
Consulate and ask them to ship us back to Paris — that is, if they won't
lend us cash. We can prove that we've got money coming to us. What
do you say?"

I didn't relish the idea, but I agreed to try. "After all, we're Americans,
aren't we? They can't let us down altogether." Something told me they
would, just the same.

When we got to the Consulate the office was filled with people. They
all looked as if they were in distress. We took a seat and waited for
the big Mogul to appear. Some people he invited into his private
office, others he dispatched on the spot. More people had entered
after us, so that the room was still crowded when at last he beckoned
to us to step up.

Mona began in her rapid, throaty way, rather confusedly, I thought. When she had half finished her speech he put up his hand and said — "Louder, if you please".

She began all over again, even more falteringly now than before. When he heard the word money he frowned and put up his hand again. At this point I decided to take over.

I had hardly begun when he interrupted to say — "Louder, please. I'm hard of hearing." Then, without waiting to hear me out, he said: "This is not a charity organization . . .". I was incensed. "I know it isn't", I said, "and we're not asking for charity. Let me . . . ."

"*Louder!*" he shouted, looking almost apoplectic now.

"We don't want you to give us money", I shouted, "we have money . . . in New York . . . to pay back whatever you lend us. If you can't lend us money, can you at least give us train tickets back to Paris?"

"To where?" he asked. "*Louder!*"

"To Paris!" I yelled.

"Can't do it", he shouted. "We're not here to take care of indigent citizens."

"We're not beggars", I shouted. "We're broke, that's all."

"Same thing", he said. "Sorry, you'll have to try elsewhere."

"Like where?" I asked.

"What?" he shouted.

"Never mind", I said. "I'll write a letter to the President. Maybe he'll lend us something out of his private pocket."

My answer was lost on the old duffer. He had already turned his back on us.

"Come on", I said, taking Mona by the elbow. "Let's get out of this filthy place. I told you we'd get nowhere with these people. The old fool! They should have retired him twenty years ago. *Louder!* Why doesn't he get an ear trumpet?"

They were highly amused, Georges and Paul, when we related our visit to them.

"Unbelievable!" said Paul.

"Bastards!" said Georges.

We voted to have a drink somewhere and wash the bad taste out of our mouths.

"Curious country", said Paul. "You give money to starving people all over the world but you can't help one another."

"Supposing we were French", I said, "and we had gone to the French Consulate ... what would have happened?"

"He would have listened politely and told you to come back in a fortnight."

"No", said Georges, "for a writer they might have done something. Not much, but he wouldn't have left you stranded. Did you tell your Consul that you were a writer?"

"He never gave me a chance", I said. "Besides, to be a writer means nothing in our country. A writer is just another bum. A poor writer, anyway."

"Funny country", said Paul. "Stay in France. We'll take better care of you."

"When do you think your money will come?" asked Georges.

I shrugged my shoulders. "It will surely come in a day or two", said Mona. "It's almost two weeks now since we wrote the bank."

"The boats are slow", said Paul. "Maybe you'll have to wait another ten days."

"I won't", said Mona. "If it doesn't come in a day or two I'll borrow the train fare to Paris from our bootblack friend."

"It's a lot of money", said Paul.

"Don't you have any friends in Paris who would send you the money?" asked Georges.

"We don't have any rich friends", I said. "Let's not worry about it any more. Something will turn up. At the last minute Providence always takes care of us. You'll see."

"We'll have to return to Arles tomorrow, said Paul. "Maybe we can borrow something from our friends there."

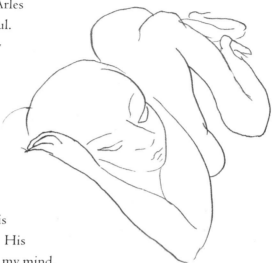

It was in Arles, while inspecting the stone sarcophagi which used to be floated down the river, that I got to think- ing of Joachim of Floris and the Third Kingdom. His name had flashed through my mind, I remember, as we passed through the strange little town of Pont St. Esprit on our way to the Pont du Gard. Fritz von Unruh had something to do with it too. Ever since Irma had dropped his name it had lodged in my brain like a tumor. *Unruh.* What a wonderful name for a poet! As she became more and more restless, I began calling Mona Madame von Unruh — to myself, of course.

We had spent a wonderful day at the Pont du Gard, one of those dreamy days when all manner of names, thoughts, ideas float through one's mind. For some strange reason this startling relic of Roman days left me thinking of the American Indian rather than the ancient Romans. There was something so sluggish, so peaceful, so dreamlike about the region that I simply could not associate it with those active busy bodies, the Romans. To my disordered mind this massive ruin of an aqueduct seemed more like the work of an unknown people, a race out of the distant past, a poetic, inspired people, who, like the Pygmies of Africa, took pleasure in their creation, and then forgot about it. And so, as I lay there by the river bank gazing up at this stupendous piece of masonry, my mind began to toy with such figures as Nicholas of Cusa, Pico della Mirandola, St. Bernard, Abelard, Francis of Assisi. and such like. Somehow, and not in the least incongruously, they blended with my dream of the American Indian, the great plains, the pueblos, the god Manitou, the elk, the moose, the buffalo.

So it was that, walking through the Aliscamps in Arles, my mind reverted to that blissful day beside the Pont du Gard, and then, like a flash, Joachim of Floris made his entry. It was in Spengler's *Decline of the West* that I first encountered his name, probably around three in the morning, while waiting for Mona and Stasia to return from their usual nocturnal peregrinations. No doubt the torment I endured during those wee hours of the morning added to my excitement when I read of his (Joachim of Floris) thoughts about the Three Kingdoms: The Age of the Law, or the Father; the Age of the Gospel, or the Son and the Age of the Spirit, which would bring all the ages to an end. (Later, much later, I was to become positively ecstatic about this Third Kingdom, the Age of the Spirit, when "the entire world would become a vast monastery, the resting season, so to speak, or the Sabbath of humanity." But that was to happen through a contemporary's writings, the Russian Berdyaev.)

It wasn't so strange, therefore, my "universalist" sort of reverie under the shadow of the ancient Pont du Gard, my fusion of humanists and red Indians, of Manitou and Zion City of our Lord. I did not know until much much later that it was in this very town of Arles in the year 1260 that Joachim's writings and supporters were condemned by the Church. How altogether fitting, this! For when has the Church ever shown evidence in the belief that one day we shall all be as Christ, that the Kingdom of Heaven is here on earth, and that when we realize it history will be no more. As I stepped into that grim, forbidding-looking church at the end of the path, suddenly I bethought me of my conversation one day at noon with the foreman of the lemon ranch where I had once worked as a ranch hand — just outside Chula Vista, California.

"How is it we never see you at church?" he began.

"Because I never go to Church."

"Are you a Jew — or an atheist?" he demanded.

"Neither. I simply have no use for churches."

"You believe in God, don't you?"

"I don't know", I replied. "It's too big a problem."

"You've got to believe first", said he. "Then God will show you the way."

"How do you make yourself believe?" I asked.

"Pray. Pray hard. Ask Him to open your eyes."

"I don't know how to pray."

"Have you ever tried?"

"Yes, when I was a boy. But I never got anywhere."

"You came from New York, didn't you?"

"Yes sir."

"A wicked city. Hard to find God in a place like that."

"Yes sir."

Pause.

"Excuse me, sir", I began, "but can you do anything about the bedbugs at the bunk house? They're eating me alive."

"We'll see about that, son. Think of God, not of bedbugs."

"I'd like to, sir, but they keep me awake all night. I can't think of anything but them."

When he left, with a veiled threat that I had better show up at meetings *or* ... . I began to think about the God of the bedbugs. Or more precisely, what part bedbugs played in the divine cosmogony. I knew he'd never forgive me, the foreman, for introducing the subject. One doesn't speak about God and bedbugs in the same breath. It was the same with Pico della Mirandola and all the great lovers of humanity. God and man were to be kept separate. As for bedbugs, whoever was responsible for their appearance on earth had better lower his head. Better to talk cactus leaves or erysipelas. As for the Sabbath of humanity, that was a pipe dream of renegades and idlers. Mass begins at seven sharp ... better be on hand, my lad!

"The End is not Yet", as Fritz von Unruh put it.

Meanwhile Madame von Unruh was getting more and more restless. She had been to the bootblack but he didn't have that kind of money to fork out. If only she could get to Paris! Then one day there came in the mail a little *mandat* from our friends in Arles; it was just enough for the fare, a single, to Paris. Not a cent to share for lunch or dinner. I took her to the station, waved goodbye, and turned back to the hotel. In the evening's mail came the check and the bankbook from New York. I immediately sent Mona a telegram and the next morning, after settling our debts — with a handsome bonus to the Black Prince — I hopped the train for Paris. It was a long ride and I wondered if Mona had found some obliging fellow traveller with whom she had shared a meal. I also wondered what Borowski would have to say when we confronted him again.

Though it was bright and sunny, ideal weather, in fact, Paris looked gray and sombre to me after the Midi. There was too much hustle and bustle, people were too high-strung, too intense, the cafés were filled

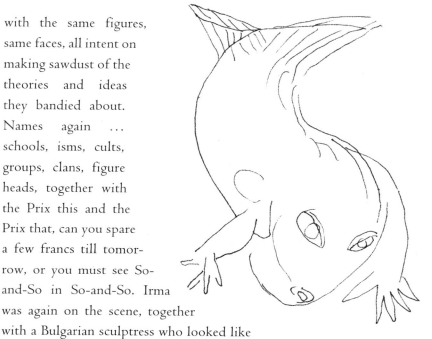

with the same figures, same faces, all intent on making sawdust of the theories and ideas they bandied about. Names again ... schools, isms, cults, groups, clans, figure heads, together with the Prix this and the Prix that, can you spare a few francs till tomorrow, or you must see So-and-So in So-and-So. Irma was again on the scene, together with a Bulgarian sculptress who looked like a mammoth sea cow. It was no longer Fritz von Unruh, or even Ernst Toller, but Brancusi, Giacometti and those Futurists from Italy, Marinetti and his meatballs who were the topic of conversation. Now and then Wyndam Lewis' name popped up, not in connection with Spengler, but with his magazine and the cult which surrounded him. I was dying to know if Irma was still pregnant, but never had a chance to pop the question. Pregnant or deflated, she seemed in high spirits. She had written some more poems, two or three of them dedicated to Mona, she said. If she could dig up the money she would return to Berlin and try to find a publisher for her poems. As for our trip, it was a pity, she averred, that we had made no effort to see Privas or Provins, why I never found out. And why hadn't we gone to Les Eyzies?

"What's there?" I asked.

"*What's there?*" she exclaimed. "Haven't you ever heard of the Cro-Magnon man?"

I nodded. Of course I had. "We'll do it the next time", I said.

"There may be no next time", she retorted.

"There's always a next time", I asserted. "It's fun to miss things. Gives you something to think about – until the next time."

"An odd way of looking at things", said Irma.

"The American way", I said, tongue in cheek. "The world is ours; all we have to do is crack it. Maybe the next time we'll be driving around in a Rolls Royce. You Germans are always afraid of missing things. That's why you carry those bloody Baedekers about with you – and your cameras and notebooks. You want to swallow everything in one gulp. Look at the French ... I'll bet you won't find a man within striking distance of us who's ever been to Les Eyzies or Provins or that other place you mentioned. Most of them have never been outside Paris. Some of them have hardly stepped foot outside their own little *arrondissement*. But they're not unhappy about it. They don't feel they've missed things. Listen, I know all about the itch which you Germans have. I've got it too in my own little way. But I'm not proud of it."

"I don't understand you", she said. "Sometimes you talk like an intelligent man and at other times you talk like a barbarian. You don't seem to have any ... what shall I say ... *respect* for things.

"You're quite right", I replied. "At bottom I don't. One thing is as good as another ... *if you're healthy*".

"Do you mean to imply that we're unhealthy?"

"In a sense, yes. I think you're contaminated by ... what shall I say (mockingly) ... by your culture? What have you gotten from your beloved idols – Homer, Aristotle, Goethe, Hegel ... ? Dyspensia, insomnia, restlessness. Always trying to prove something, always trying to change the world, but never yourselves. We're just over one war and soon you'll be leading us into another. What is it you want? You don't know. You simply don't know how to get along, either with your neighbors or with yourselves."

"You're talking about a certain type of German", she said, annoyed to be bracketed with the warmongers and Huns.

"Am I?" I said. "Are you so sure?"

"I may be a German", she said, "but my spirit is cosmopolitan".

"And I'm an American", I responded, "and what spirit I have tells me that it's all a farce. Yesterday you were the enemy, tomorrow you may be our ally. When the bugle blows we'll march, every mother's son of us, whether we are cosmopolitan in spirit or chauvinist, whether it's for the right cause or the wrong cause. I don't give a shit for any country or for any idea you may propose to save the world. This Culture which has spread through us like a poison will keep us fighting until there is no Culture left. Unfortunately there'll be no one here to enjoy Christmas on earth. The Sabbath of humanity will be for the musk-rat and the weasel, not for the likes of us."

"You sound like a Nihilist", said Irma. "If I had ideas lik shoot myself."

"That's what I do every day. But it doesn't work."

She ignored this remark as unworthy of attention.

"And when you get back home you'll write about it ... about Europe and her culture ... won't you?"

"Maybe I will and maybe I won't. My problem is *to write*, not what about."

"I don't understand", she said. "To write you have to have something to write about, isn't that so?"

"Yes and no", I replied. "But let's not get into it."

Paris was getting on my nerves more and more. Perhaps not Paris itself but the people we seemed obliged to associate with. We were always running into the same types one meets in Greenwich Village: fairies (usually poets or dancers), Lesbians (usually painters or sculptors), run down journalists (usually correspondents for some foreign paper of no consequence), young, would-be artists with long hair and dirty fingernails who would hang on for hours just to get a sandwich and a beer, spinsters who insisted on dragging us to museums, art galleries and five o'clock teas, schoolteachers from Iowa or Wisconsin who doted on authors and painters long forgotten, and so on. We never seemed to meet any French people, or at least never together. If we were parted for a few hours I was certain to hear that she had just run into some famous individual, like Brancusi or Soutine, and always by accident of course. The only person I enjoyed talking to was Carl, whom I saw rarely.

The trip to the Midi had given me a taste for another atmosphere. There it didn't matter whom I struck up a conversation with, it was always interesting. They had the gift of the gab, these men of the South. They had the sun in their bowels and that divine insouciance

which comes from basking in the sun. And everywhere there was color. Even the names of the villages were exciting, and so utterly bizarre that at times one had the impression they had been translated from Eyptian hieroglyphs or some forgotten language from the lost continent of Mu. Everywhere there was a sea of vineyards which stretched out to infinity ... That was France for me, not Paris and its environs.

Since we now had enough money to last us a while I suggested that we think about seeing some other countries. Every day spent sitting with the derelicts whom we attracted like flies was a day lost, in my opinion.

"What about a trip down the Rhine and then to Vienna and Budapest?" said Mona.

"Don't forget Romania. *Romania, Romania, Romania!* For some unknown reason I was more eager to see Romania than any of the other countries. Besides, Czernowitz, where her relatives lived, was close to the Russian border. Maybe we could have a peek at Russia too!

A few days later we crossed the German border — was it at Aachen ... What a name for Aix-la-Chapelle! There at the border the cleaning women poured into the car and, as they deposited their pails and scrubbing brushes, they yelled: "Now you are in Germany where everything is clean". And with that they fell to like dizzy demons.

The sight of them making things clean disgusted me. At once I took a dislike to Germany. Too much like home, with mother rubbing a moist finger over the wainscoting and saying – "You forgot to dust here!" As we waited on a siding for the German crew to take over, train after train of low boxcars passed us, the workmen all nude to the waist, shovelling away like mad, the very picture of work for work's sake.

As we made our way inland the train soon filled with business men and bankers buried in their newspapers, all properly washed and groomed, all loaded with cigars and pipes. It wasn't difficult to strike up a conversation; every one, moreover, seemed to speak a good English. But what dull conversations! I felt that I was back home amidst my German-American nobodies, except for the fact that these birds had a superior air, not arrogant exactly, but condescending. They were all struck from the same mould, it seemed, whether stockbrokers, jobbers, industrialists, engineers, bankers or woollen salesmen. Such a contrast to the French who were individuals first and foremost, and then work-horses of one sort or another. But rebellious work-horses. Always endeavouring to find the easiest way of doing things. But these stolid citizens gave the impression of knowing nothing but work, of taking pride in being in harness. And fearful of looking shabby or unkempt.

Slowly we made our way down the Rhine, gazing at the castles just like any other tourists. At Bonn I remember searching for Beethoven's home. And putting up for the night in a *pension* run by a most respectable widow who had seen better days. She too rubbed me the wrong way. Over coffee and Kuchen (indigestible stuff) she discoursed on the poets and philosophers of old, on the history of Germany and its marvellous system of education, all as if reading from

a book. Now and then she would politely ask about things American, only to dismiss the subject almost immediately and meander again through the cultural byways of her beloved Germany. Fortunately Mona had to bear the brunt of it, since she had a working knowledge of the language. I sat back, pretending not to understand a word.

Finally came the inevitable question – "And what does your husband do?"

When she heard that I was a writer, a *Schriftsteller*, her eyes opened wide like an owl's. I had to bear the full gaze of her Olympian scrutiny. I felt like saying, but succeeded in restraining myself: "Go on, you sour looking bitch, give me the once over and be done with it! You're looking at a monstrosity who doesn't give a fart for your Hegel, Heine, Schlegel, Fichte, Dichter, Doktor, Tochter or Faustus. Beneath this callow hide everything is clean as a whistle: no idealism, no nominalism, no realism, no Katzenellenbogism. Pure as the driven snow … a clean slate … empty as a pisspot. Won't ever make the grade, if that's what you're wondering about. Don't put the music on … I know it all backwards. Isn't it lovely to chat every day with some new visitor from abroad? Yes, it's a wonderful country, *Deutschlan —* *abernicht 'uber alles'.* Luther, you say? I'll trade him for John Brown — you know, the hero of Harper's Ferry. Or Daniel Boone."

She seemed to get it telepathically, the dried up prune. "He must be a very interesting writer indeed", she said to Mona as she ushered us out of the dining room. What she meant was — "Don't ever bring that man in here again, *please."*

In Cologne all I remember besides the Cathedral was the abominable meal of cold cuts and potato salad. And the serious, the deadly serious way in which the diners sat eating their food.

"Let's get on", I said, "This country is driving me nuts".

As we sauntered down the street suddenly from an open window there came a burst of piano music which stopped me in my tracks.

"Do you hear that?" I said, while from another window came the voice of a Gadski practising the scales. "That's something we never heard in France. Never any music while walking the streets. This is wonderful. Let's stand and listen a while. What is it he's playing ... is it Brahms? Yeah, music they have, the bastards. Good music too. But where does it come from? Where do they dig it up? They all look like dressed up vegetables, yet they have music in their souls. I don't understand that guy who's knocking out Brahms, for all you know he may be a lieutenant in the artillery. I can see the soldier in them, but I'm damned if I can see the poet or the musician. Maybe it's the beer that inspires them."

"Wait till you get to Vienna", said Mona. "It'll be like drinking champagne."

Suddenly I had a thought. "Before
we leave this bloody country
I'd like to visit Darmstadt
and see if I can find
out anything about
my   grandfather,
Valentin
Nieting.   What
do you say?"

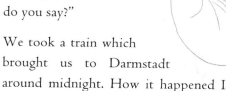

We took a train which
brought   us   to   Darmstadt
around midnight. How it happened I
don't know, but at the station we fell into conversation with the
station master, a big, good-natured idiot dressed like a horse and
wagon. We had begun by asking the name of a hotel, when suddenly
he said: "And what brings you to Darmstadt at this time of night?"
Whereupon I told him of my grandfather. "No need to go any
further", he said. "We have the books here. Let me look up his name."

After waiting twenty minutes or more, while he thumbed through the
directories, he informed me that there was no such name as Nieting
in the books. "Maybe he lived in some village nearby."

Then and there I lost my appetite. The idea of going on a wild goose
chase in search of the long dead Valentin Nieting struck me as absurd.

"Let's take the next train out of here", I said. "Let's get on to Vienna."

On we went. Was it the next morning or the morning after that, I no
longer remember, but waking up out of a sound snooze I looked out
the window and there before my eyes was a scene right out of Breughel.

"We're in the Tyrol now", said Mona.

"*The Tyrol*? God, this is heavenly. Too good to be true."

I sat and stared at the changing scene, as we wound in and around the mountain passes. Absolutely enchanting, it was. Why not get out somewhere and forget Vienna for a while? "Yeah, why not get out at the next stop?" I said.

"We can't", she replied. "They'll be waiting for us at the station."

"Who will?"

"My uncle and aunt. I told you we would have to stay with them for a while."

It was a let down, Vienna, after the beautiful Tyrol. All seemed grim, desolate, threadbare. Maybe it was only like that around the station, I thought to myself. Don't judge too hastily.

Her uncle was there waiting for us, his face wreathed in smiles. He looked haggard, shabbily clothed, anything but the Colonel of the Hussars he once had been. He wouldn't let us take a taxi, too expensive, he said. We took a tram and then a bus. We walked down a lugubrious looking street that might have been lifted out of Greenpoint, Brooklyn, except that in Greenpoint the walls of the buildings showed no signs of being sprayed by bullets.

Up three flights of stairs through ill-smelling halls, the linoleum worn to tatters, the wainscoting hanging in shreds. We came to a door whose varnish had long since peeled off; there was a little brass sign above the doorbell with his name on it. He pushed the button and in a moment his wife appeared, followed by their young daughter.

It was a warm, tearful reception we received. To think that we had come all the way from America to see them! What questions they plied us with! Every few minutes her Aunt burst into renewed spasms of joy and grief. What they couldn't get over was how beautiful Mona looked, how much she resembled her grand-mother from Buk-ovina. Later they would make us go through the family album. First we had to have some coffee and cake. Then it would be time for lunch. But first the Colonel had to do a few errands. She meant by that some stupid job, one of several that he had taken on. But he would be back in an hour or so.

We were taken through the apartment. Our valises were stacked in the bedroom. Was the place suitable? she wondered aloud. To her it was unthinkable that we lived in anything but luxury.

I urged Mona to tell her quickly that we intended to put up at a hotel but she shushed me down. "We can't do that immediately", she whispered. "They would be offended."

For me it was like being back in Williamsburg. The same old furniture from the year One, same drapes, doilies, insane pictures, often in mica, same bedspreads ... even a cuspidor or two. The best thing in the place was the stove, a huge affair in porcelain which intrigued me no end. I prayed that we would be able to clear out in a day or two.

The daughter was a charming creature of thirteen or fourteen who already knew a little English. The Colonel, of course, spoke it quite fluently. He had been a handsome man in his day and evidently possessed of unusual qualities. Now his teeth were rotting away, he had grown quite bald, and he suffered from all sorts of ailments. The worst was that he could find no decent employment. What he was doing a boy of twelve could have done just as well. His principal work was to deliver reels from one movie house to another. He also acted as janitor for the building. Between times he delivered newspapers. And with all his jobs he had a devil of a time paying the rent. As for shoes and clothing, these they came by in miraculous ways. Anna, the daughter, was the best dressed. At that, she looked to me like someone who had just stepped out of an orphan asylum. They were not morose, however. On the contrary, they seemed quite gay, quite cheerful. They had accepted their condition. Who hadn't? There was nothing else to do.

After lunch, which was quite generous considering their circumstances, the Colonel asked me if I played chess. I told him I was a very bad player but would be happy to give him a game. He seemed inordinately pleased. Evidently that was the only thing he could afford to do in his spare time. Mona meanwhile accompanied the aunt and daughter on a shopping tour.

I realized after a few moves that I was no match for my host. I suggested that he give me a rook and a bishop next game, He didn't like to do that, he said. If I wished he would teach me a little about the strategy of the game. I consented.

As we shuffled the pieces about he told me about Napoleon, what a poor player he was despite his extraordinary knowledge of military strategy. He then went on to talk of von Molkte and of Robert E. Lee, for whom he had the highest respect, not only as a military man but as an individual. I was somewhat surprised at this, but even more surprised when he began talking of Alexander and the battles that had made him famous.

We played again that night, after he had collected and delivered all the reels, after he had put the garbage cans out and attended to all the other little chores connected with his daily routine. There was something Chaplinesque about him. To look at him he was a nobody; less than a nobody, in fact. He performed his humble duties seriously and punctiliously, as if his life depended on it, which it did, to be truthful. But the moment he entered the home he was another man ... not just an ex-Colonel of his Majesty's Death's Head Hussars, but a gentleman of breeding, a man of culture, a man who would have attracted attention in a salon, even such a one as Madame de Stael's.

It was a tough night, that first one. I had hardly dozed off when I was aware of something biting me. I turned on the light and to my horror I saw columns of bedbugs and cockroaches streaming up and down the walls. Naturally neither of us hardly slept a wink.

"We've got to get out of here quick", I said.

After breakfast Mona gently broke the news that we intended to take a hotel. To my consternation the aunt wouldn't hear of it.

"Tell her about the bugs", I said.

"I can't, Val. I wouldn't hurt her feelings for the world."

She pleaded some more, Mona, whereupon it was agreed that in a week or so we might take other quarters. No mention of the bugs, however.

It was difficult even to go for a walk alone. They were afraid we might get lost. We managed to take a little jaunt with Anna, the daughter, but it was hardly a promenade. The little we saw was scarcely inviting. Nothing but tenement houses, sad-looking Bier-Stube, butcher shops

and grocery shops even more dilapidated looking than one finds in the ghettos of New York. I hadn't the slightest idea where we were in this vast city. I knew only that we were among the very poor.

The Colonel had promised that come Sunday he would take us for a stroll in the evening. He would get someone to substitute for him, he said. Meanwhile it was the same routine night and day. Chess, bugs, military strategy, reminiscences of the war and after the war, plus a constant feeling of itchiness, sleepiness, restlessness.

One can get used to cockroaches but not bedbugs. How we stood it the ten days we spent with them I no longer understand. Somehow the days passed, and the nights too, though the nights were intolerably long.

Sunday came and we went for the long promised tour of the neighborhood. It seemed to me that we were following a canal. Wherever we were it was poorly lighted. We entered a little café whose light was hardly more brilliant than the street light. In the corner, wrapped in a web like one of the Fates, sat a wizened old woman plucking at the zither. She sang in a cracked, weary voice which was not only melancholy but sinister and lugubrious. The clients sat about with heads bowed, as if doing penitence. The beer was warm and the flies quickly collected on the rims of the glasses. I began to itch more than ever.

When we hit the street and had walked a few paces I perceived that we were in some low quarter taken over by the whores of yesterday. They were worse than the flies, I soon found out. It didn't matter to them that we were accompanied by our wives and a girl in her teens. They swarmed all over us, clutching our arms, trying to drag us to a bar ... we could at least buy them a drink, could we not?

I had had my fill of gazing at Grosz' *Ecce Homo*, which Mona had brought from Paris the previous year. I had accepted the fact that the Germans after their defeat could not have been far different from the monsters which Grosz had portrayed. But I had never given a thought to Vienna and the other cities of Europe which had suffered a like fate. It was now ten years after the defeat of the German forces, moreover. It might have been yesterday, for all that spoke of change here. Never have I seen such whores, such sinister looking alleyways, such utter despair and hopelessness written into the faces of human beings. I wondered why he had led us into such a quarter. It was for the simple reason, he soon explained, that we should know something about the misery of the European. He wanted this picture to remain in our minds; he wanted us to tell our friends about it when we got home. The war was bad enough, he said, but after the war ... that was still worse. Nobody had a right to live in luxury, not even we Americans. There must be a revolution, he said, a revolution that would sweep the earth clean. "We haven't the strength to start a revolution", he said. "It must come from a country like yours. Give us something to hope for. Help us get rid of these crafty politicians, these insane militarists. Get us food and clothing, homes to live in, give us another system of education. We are hardly human beings any more. If I die tomorrow, what will become of my wife and child? Are they to go on the street, like these poor creatures you saw tonight? Help us! Speak to your countrymen! Here nobody listens. We have only one hope – to die in bed and not in the gutter."

That night I didn't sleep a wink. It wasn't the bedbugs that kept me awake, it was Europe, the horror and misery, which penetrated it through and through. "Speak to your countrymen!" How little he knew America! One might as well talk to a stone wall. Not that there weren't thousands of good souls who were aiding the poor Europeans, usually those who had little to spare, but revolution ... didn't he realize that that word was taboo in America? Even a revolution abroad. No, America didn't want to see a clean sweep made of it. America was just as anachronistic in her ideas as any other country. America wanted improvements, yes, a rise in the standard of living sufficient to gain us more customers. We had goods to sell, not ideas. When the Europeans had acquired a decent standard of living we would have other things to sell them, such as rifles, cannons, tanks, gas masks and what not. Never mention the word revolution! We had rather see them starve first ... .

The following afternoon we visited the Prater together. That was fun. Fun in a civilized setting, something unknown to me in America. In America, of course, we had no benign or mad monarchs, no dukes, princes and so forth to bequeath to the public their magnificent estates. Coney Island, which every European seems to have heard of and would like to visit some day, is not the creation of a madman but of a mobster. Strolling through the Prater I had the feeling of rejoining my forefathers; I could now understand why, as a child, the picnics and excursions the old folks had provided for us could no longer be duplicated. "Far away and long ago." With us "the vulgar advent", as Nostradamus calls it, began with the turn of the century. Perhaps in Arkansas, Minnesota, Idaho one might still be able to enjoy such simple pastimes, but never, even in those places, in an ambiance such as the Prater.

Finally we managed to persuade her relatives to let us clear out. The day before leaving Mona arrived with two stout fellows laden with supplies. Her aunt wept when she saw what Mona had selected for them. There was everything under the sun, from food and liquor to pots and pans. Enough to last out a siege. In addition she slipped them some cash, a not inconsiderable amount, as I soon learned. It might be necessary, she said, unless we had a windfall (meaning Pop) to curtail our vacation. On the impulse I wanted to say – "Let's give them all we have but our fare home. Let's cut it short right here." But then I quickly realized that it was no solution to their problem. A few months of luxury and they would be right back where we had found them. The solution was for Anna to find a rich husband — from Argentina or Cambodia or the wilds of Texas.

We found a modest hotel in the center of town, somewhere near the Ring. The first thing we did, of course, was to take a steaming bath and examine one another for lice, bedbugs, cockroaches and other vermin. We had examined the bed carefully — stripped it, that is — immediately on being shown our room. Not a sign of insect life. It was a huge, soft bed, moreover, in which it was a pleasure to repose.

One day, while wandering about, it suddenly occurred to me that somewhere in the vicinity must be the Hotel Mueller, where Mona had stayed with that handsome young chap the year before. Am Grabe, I remember she had said it was. I decided I would have a look at the place, see if I could examine the hotel register. I entered the lobby, looked about casually, as if I had a rendezvous with someone, all the while wondering how I could persuade the clerk to let me glance through the register. Just as I had acquired the necessary courage, just as I got within a foot or two of the desk and about to open my mouth, I realized that I no longer remembered the name of her handsome young friend. I assumed that they would have registered as Mr and Mrs So-and-So. (Which they wouldn't, not if they had to show their passports, which they certainly must have done.) But all this I only thought of later. I ended up by asking the clerk the price of a room, a huge double room with private bath and all the trimmings, in order to impress him. This was a mistake, because before I knew it I was in the elevator being escorted to the bridal suites. He had evidently spotted me for an American, probably the son of a millionaire who was modestly attired in order not to attract attention to himself. It took me half-an-hour to get out of the damned hotel. I left assuring him that my wife and I would telephone in a day or two, that the rooms were exactly to our taste, and I was certain that the restaurant would be the same. With all the bowing and scraping I found myself backing out of the hotel bowing and nodding with the same ridiculous ceremony.

On the way home I ran into an attractive prostitute whom I found it difficult to elude without first having a little drink somewhere. This somewhere was in the most expensive hotel in Vienna, one that the Kaiser himself used to frequent. We had a long talk over our expensive drinks, during which I tried my damndest to convince her that I was impotent. It took her no time to demonstrate that this was a fib. Not only did she deftly and discreetly massage me under the table but with a boldness that terrified me she managed to open my fly and fish it out. There I was, in the Kaiser's plush hotel, stuttering and blushing, a drink in my trembling hand, endeavoring to look nonchalant as the waiters passed, while this cool practised bitch masturbated me without let. Needless to say there was no need to look for a room. She understood that too. All that was left to do was to button my fly and hand her some dough. As we parted down the street somewhere she remarked: "Next time we meet you won't get away so easily". With that she put her arms around me and gave me a warm kiss.

When I got back to the hotel I pleaded a headache and dove into bed. I slept like a rock — until dinnertime.

After dinner, while searching for a cosy cafe, Mona had the bright idea to lead me to the Graben and point out the Hotel Dueller. "That's the place Ron and I stayed at", she said. "Do you remember me telling you about it?"

"I sure do", I said. "Looks like a rather expensive joint."

"Not at all", she replied. "I don't think my room came to more than three dollars."

"And what about *his* room?"

111

"Are you trying to trip me up
again?" Mona said, with
a twinkle in her eye.
"All you have to
do is go in and
look up the
register."

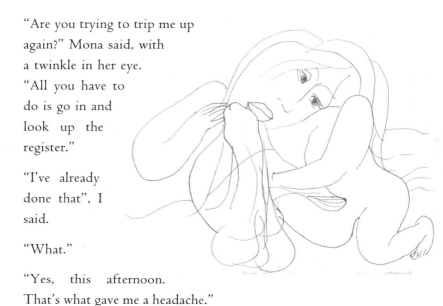

"I've already
done that", I
said.

"What."

"Yes, this afternoon.
That's what gave me a headache."

"I don't believe you."

"Go in and ask the room clerk", I said. "He'll remember me. I
promised we'd come there in a day or two. I selected one of the bridal
suites."

'You're absolutely mad, Val. Besides, I may as well tell you now ...
Ron was a homosexual. Maybe he was bisexual. But he never attracted
me that way. I went on that because I was angry with Stasia for running
off to Africa without me."

"You might have told me all that before. Anyway, what difference
does it make? That was last year. Next year ..." I checked myself. I
was just about to say, "Next year it will be someone else". No need to
put ideas into her head.

We stayed on at the same hotel a few days longer, then decided it was
time to move on. We counted our money carefully and estimated that,

if we indulged in no nonsense, we could see Budapest and Czernowitz and then home. As a precautionary measure Mona dispatched a letter to Pop saying that her funds were dwindling and could he send an additional sum to her at the American Express, Paris, in the next three or four weeks. She added that she had been staying with her relatives in Vienna, that they were miserably poor, and that she had foolishly perhaps given them a good slice of her vacation money. Always adroit, Mona, in blending truth and fiction. She felt certain, she said, that Pop wouldn't let her down. He was not like Borowski.

Before leaving for Hungary we had a last meal with Mona's relatives in a restaurant which they selected. We were a bit concerned about the language problem, naturally. The Colonel tried to assure us that with German and English we would have no problem. Just the same I persuaded him to write out a few phrases for us in Hungarian. Simple things like – "Where is the nearest Post Office?" "How much does this cost?" "What time is it, please?" "Where is the men's toilet?" "I beg pardon!" "Can you give me light, please?" "May I see the menu?" And so on. He wrote the sentences out painstakingly, accents and all, and pronounced them over and over, which was meaningless because the next instant I forgot how to say even the simplest expression. What a language! What an impossible language! For example: 'Bocsanatot Kerek.' Could anyone but a Hungarian possibly know that this meant 'Excuse me, please!' Or this – to see the menu: 'Kernem Az Etlapot!' As for 'How much does this cost?' (Mennyibe Kerulez?). Only a wizard could get the drift of it. With my bladder bursting and a look of desperation in my eye, I was soon to find out what a jam one could get into asking the way to the watercloset. I mention this because this was one of the (very necessary) phrases I had done my best to memorize. Came the moment and the bloody words dropped completely out of my mind. Dancing on one leg, then the other, I fished out my notebook, repeated it to myself a half-dozen times, then looked about for someone to try it on. As luck would have it, the man was drunk. Besides, he wasn't Hungarian but Polish, and a brute to boot. "Hol Van A Ferfi Closet?" I repeated three times. He shook his head, asked me something in Polish, to which I shook my head in turn, and turned his back on me. I went after him, clutched him by the sleeve and, looking at him imploringly, I held my balls in one hand and with the other made as if to piss. A dull light gleamed in his ox-like countenance. "Pissy", he said. Or that's what it sounded like. "Yes", I said, getting more and more frantic. "*Pissy!*" He grabbed me by the arm and lurching to and fro escorted me to the place. As I pushed open the door I noticed that it was clearly written "Men's Room". "Pissy!" he shouted. "Good, *pissy!*" I already had my cock out, pissing like mad, when he opened the door, peeked in and said: "Good!" I waved with my free hand and shouted "*Muchas gracias!*"

Of course it was just like the Colonel had said. With Mona's German we found that we could make our way about quite easily. It was late morning when the train pulled in to Budapest. We hopped a cab and told the driver to lead us to a modest hotel – a clean one. He chose a beauty, it seemed to me, on the edge of a big square. Instantly I fell in love with Budapest. It sparkled. There was catnip in the air.

The room we were given faced the square; it was a beautiful view from the huge French windows which we immediately opened; we stepped out on the balcony to get a better view. Suddenly I bethought me of the bed. "Have you looked at the bed yet?" I asked.

"No", said Mona, why? It looks alright to me."

"Have you looked inside?" I said, making a grimace. Immediately she pulled back the covers, and immediately we discovered what we didn't want to see – our dear inseparable friends, the bedbugs. Only two or three, but who knew how many more lurked in the mattress?

I pulled the bell cord and in a few moments the porter appeared. I took him to the bed and showed him the bedbugs. There were only two visible now. He didn't seem to be too upset by the discovery. In a few minutes he led us to another room, even larger, even more handsomely furnished, and for the same price. I wondered what the hitch was. We took the bed apart under his eyes, pulled out all the bureau drawers, examined the clothes closet thoroughly, and satisfied that there were no bugs about, we tipped him again and started unpacking. As she was unpacking, Mona, out fell two bedbugs — dead ones, fortunately. We examined each and every article of clothing we had before putting them away. We took another bath, just to make sure, doused ourselves with toilet water, and changed our clothes.

I still felt itchy, but I said nothing. The bedbugs were now in our minds, much harder to get rid of than those to be found in a bed. In eating I noticed that we first examined our food, prodding it this way and that, to make sure no bugs had found their way into it. Sometimes the whole meal hour passed in discussing the difference between the various kinds of pests, their looks, smell, habits, habitat, etc. To make certain that none of these vicious bugs which we may have swallowed inadvertently, whether dead or alive, would cause us harm, we consumed quantities of Hunyadi Janos, which was probably death to germs of any kind but also rough on the bowels. I learned to say *Au revoir* in Hungarian, not in parting from friends but in parting from the bugs. A marvellous word, if you don't choke on it. "Viszontlatasra!"

Almost the first thing I was aware of, in strolling about, was the elegance of the men's attire. They knew how to dress, the Hungarians. Such a contrast to the Germans and the French. The language, of course, seemed only to enhance their sense of elegance; a man in a cutaway with gloves, spats and cane could only express himself in the language of the poet, utterly unintelligible though it sounded to my ears. The city itself, especially viewed from the heights of Buda, looked elegant.

In Buda was the Matjaskirche, the like of which I had never seen. For once I had found a church which breathed gaiety. It was alive with color, as if decorated by flamingos and peacocks rather than human beings. Also up there on the heights of Buda were the thermal baths, some of them dating back to Roman times. The town itself was not spectacular; it seemed neglected in comparison with Pest. But it was from Buda that one could appreciate the beauty of Pest and of Margaret Island which lay between the two cities.

It was inevitable that we should again have dealings with the Gypsies. They were all over the place, like the bedbugs in the hotels. We had become more wary of them now; instead of twenty dollar bills we offered ones. It was difficult indeed not to empty one's pockets after one of these swarthy oily devils had crept up to your table and, as if

with the fingers of a demented angel, played in your ear. Every one of these devils played like a virtuoso. They were born with a fiddle in their hands. To give oneself up completely to the music was to risk madness. All the sorrows, woes, misery, melancholy, despair and longing of the human race was embraced in their wild melodies. It was certainly not the music of the concert hall; it was the music of the blood, the music of the wanderer, the outcast, the exile, the homeless, rootless man. It spoke with an icy frenzy, and always of passions, instincts, lusts that had been bottled and contained for centuries. Each time it broke out it awakened the archaic man, the collective being which sang before it spoke, which danced before it declaimed, which made music before it made houses, streets, fortresses and castles. Which sang the glory of the heavens before ever the heavens were charted.

117

A weird, walled off-race, these savage artists. So smooth and slippery, so unctuous, so fierce, so utterly disaffiliated with the rest of humanity, their only defense against the cruel onslaughts of a hostile world being their instruments, their vocal chords, their magical ability to charm the devil himself. One could never feel sorry for a Gypsy; he was beyond the reach of sympathy or compassion. Nor could one feel annoyed or irritated should he drain one of his last penny. One could be wary, nothing more. If one had to be robbed of his last cent the best was to ask for a slow, lingering bloodletting. It seemed to me, as I sat bewitched, that it was only natural that this anomalous element of humanity should flourish here in the midst of elegance and finesse, amidst men and women speaking with the tongues of snakes and the blades of broken daggers. "Szabadna Egy Kistuzet, Kewem?" (Can you give me a light, please?) "*Kszonom Szepen!*" (Thank you very much!)

"Let's walk a bit", I said, as we hit the street. "My head's on fire. *Aztublyienem cigarootzl*? Excuse me, will you, if I talk a little Hungarian. I want to get the firecrackers out of my bung hole. How did you like those little toads they served with the paprika? And that cabinet minister with the huge wart on his eyelid ... did you notice? They were drinking Slivovitz, if I'm not mistaken. Vile stuff. But that violinist, the one who played in your ear ... did you ever see a more sinister looking scoundrel? He'll keep them merry in the depths of hell. I don't feel itchy anymore, do you? My spine is all aflame. We ought to find a quiet little spot and have some beer. Now the zither would sound soothing, don't you think? The zither with a dash of paprika, what! Your uncle must just be returning from his last delivery now. And Sid Essen, bless his heart, must be snoring his head off. Jesus, but wouldn't he go mad if he had to listen to that music? I must send him a postcard tomorrow. And Ulric too. I don't think Ulric ever got to Budapest. He was more interested in the Italian primitives. Thank God we don't have to visit any museums ... ."

I looked at her but there was no response. She was too choked up, I guess, to venture a word.

We walked a little further and, just as we caught sight of a café, I broke out again.

"The funniest thought just occurred to me. Are you listening?"

"Yes, Val."

"I was thinking of Moskowitz down on Second Avenue … the cymbalon … the box of candy he bought every night … and that banker, what's his name again, you had on the string then? Remember? He used to travel a lot, if I remember right. Would be funny to run into him in a town like this … or in some god-awful hole like Moldavitza or whatever you call it, eh? Wonder what ever became of him? And Ulric saying to me – 'You'll get there one day, never fear'. And now we're here. Here and not here. You know what I mean? Sometimes I feel completely dismembered. We've already taken in more than we can digest. Never dreamed, did you, when you were trotting around with those imported candies, that you'd be walking the streets of Budapest one day? Maybe one day we'll be walking around in Lhasa. Who knows? If I had the money I'd take one of those Gypsies along, have him play for us when we felt moody. We wouldn't need to worry about going broke then. Jesus, what idiots we must have been walking our legs off from one dive to another with a suitcase full of imported candies! I should have learned to play the harmonica at least. When you think of it, there isn't a damned thing we know how to do, is there?"

I gave her another glance. Still silent. I thought I saw a tear glistening in the corner of her eye. But I had to go on. The music was wailing in the roots of my hair.

"I suppose we've got *something*, or we wouldn't be here. The devil's luck, perhaps. You know, every time you tell someone that your husband is a writer I feel like crawling into a hole. If I could write like those guys fiddle I'd be the happiest man alive. There's one thing certain, no one is born with pen in hand. These bloody devils learned to play without reading a note. Imagine a writer not knowing the alphabet! And even when you *can* spell, even when you *can* put words together, it doesn't mean you're a writer. To write you have to have the itch. And I've been itchy ever since I was born. Tonight, listening to that music, I got a strange feeling of confidence. I may still find the way to say what I want to say. Maybe I'll write in Hungarian. Like that I'll be able to go off the deep end .... ."

We took a seat in a sleepy little joint. The waiter was a hunchback from Bavaria who might have been sired by one of the gargoyles from Notre Dame. He took us to be British and we let it go at that. Every few minutes he reappeared to light our cigarettes. Once he asked if we liked horses; he knew where we could rent a pair if we wished to go riding. I told him I had never been near a horse, that I was a chess player. I made the jumps that a knight makes – on an imaginary board. He brought us two more beers. "In your honor", he said, in perfect English. "I used to play in Battersea Park." Then, not to dismiss him too abruptly, I asked how to say – 'Where is the nearest Post Office?' I already had it in my notebook, but I wanted to hear how it sounded. "Hol Van A Legkozelebbi Postahivatal?"

"Please don't ask him any more questions", said Mona. "We'll never get him off our hands."

"Okay. Now what was I saying a minute ago? Oh yeah, about the music .... . The thing is to do it, whether you know how or not. That's what I was trying to tell you. Anybody can put words together. Language, ordinary language, is just a washboard. Writing is something else. It's like a perpetual cadenza on the edge of a precipice. So far I haven't written a line. I've been scrubbing clothes, dirty clothes. First I've got to find out who I am, where I came from, where I'm going, why I'm here. I've got to make myself an orphan, teach myself my own language, stop taking music lessons and all that. First I've got to get rid of all the baggage I've accumulated ... I mean *literature*. That Gypsy taught me more in a few minutes than all the volumes of Henry James, Dostoievsky, Knut Hamsun and Peter Schlemiehl combined. So far I've just been doing homework, that's what. And giving myself good grades behind the teacher's back. What I need is a good, swift kick in the ass ... By the way, how long do you want to stay here?"

"It's up to you, Val", she replied. "What's the matter? Are you getting restless? I thought you liked Budapest?"

"I do, but I don't want to hang on indefinitely. I think we should pull up stakes soon ... get on to Czernowitz ... see a little of Russia, if we can. What do you say?"

"Whatever you like Val. But don't worry about finances, please. I'm sure there'll be money waiting for us in Paris when we get back. Pop won't let me down."

"Listen, I know you don't like me to talk about it, but do you honestly think that Pop swallows all this stuff you hand him?"

"I don't think about it", she replied. "That's his look-out."

"I wish I could look at things that way. I always wonder what goes on in people's minds, even when it's just a simple conversation I'm having with them. I suppose it's because I'm talking three different ways at once sometimes. Maybe people are less complicated than I imagine."

"You're a writer", she said. "It's only natural to think the way you do."

I bent forward. "Now and then I wish you'd say something else when people ask you what I do. Can't you say, like I did just now, that I'm a chess player . . . or maybe a veterinarian?"

"Of course I can, if you want it that way. But I don't see why."

"It's more fun the other way, that's all. It makes me feel less responsible. Sometimes, b'Jesus, I wish I were nothing but a chess player, or even a shoemaker. The minute you say you're a writer something happens. People expect you to deliver golden apples or something. They're no longer natural. You get the feeling that you have to prove something. Because the first thought in people's minds is — is he a good writer or a bad writer? Is he a genius or is he a dud? You see what I mean?"

"No, Val, I don't. But then I'm not a writer."

"Let's drop it. I'm probably talking through my hat. Tell me a little about your relatives in Romania. What does your uncle do? He's your mother's brother, isn't he? Or is it your father's?"

"I've told you a dozen times", she replied. "You don't listen. Frankly, I don't know anything about them. All I know is that they're fairly well off."

"That means no bedbugs, I hope!"

She smiled. "I wouldn't guarantee it, Val. Bedbugs seem to make no distinction between rich and poor . . . in Europe."

"In *Central* Europe, you mean. I'm sure they don't have them in the Scandinavian countries. I wonder who introduced them . . . the Huns? Well, we'll still have the Gypsies, won't we? That'll make up for any hardships we have to endure."

Two days later we said goodbye to Budapest. It was a long ride to the Romanian border. We took a third-class compartment, with wooden benches, in order to economize. The compartment we occupied was filled with Jews. Poor Jews, who looked as if they were fleeing from the Cossacks. It wasn't long before we made friends with them, shared our food,  and so on. They were very inquisitive about America, thought it a wonderful haven of refuge. If only they could get there one day! In their eyes we were, like all Americans, rich. They couldn't resist feeling the texture of our clothes, examining our shoes, inquiring the price of this article and that.

All of a sudden, at a train stop, the door slid open with a bang and there stood a man and woman, evidently of the upper class, glowering at us as if we were a bunch of hoodlums.

"Get up!" said the man in Polish, fixing one of the Jews. He looked at each of us in turn as if we were holding out on him. "Get up and give the lady a seat!"

Nobody budged.

"What did he say?" I asked my neighbor.

"He wants us to get out. He's a Pole. A Count, maybe."

"Don't do a thing", I said.

"He'll make trouble for us", whispered the Jew, squirming in his seat.

I turned to Mona. "Tell him in German that there's no room."

She did. He pretended not to understand.

"*You* tell him", I said to my neighbor.

But he was afraid to open his mouth. I glanced from one to another. I could see that they were all fear and trembling.

"Disgraceful!" I said to myself. Then, in English, I spoke to them. The man meanwhile had left the doorway but his wife was still standing there. I said: "Don't be frightened. You have a right to your place and you're going to keep your place. Let him do what he likes."

I had hardly finished when the "Count" — a towering figure, by the way, enough to inspire fear in anyone — returned with the conductor. We had to show our tickets, each and every one. Satisfied that all was in order, the conductor shrugged his shoulders and started to move off. The "Count" detained him by the arm. He spoke rapidly and angrily, as if telling him what to do. Evidently he was telling him that one of these dirty Jews ought to have the decency to surrender his seat to a lady. The conductor shrugged his shoulders again and marched off, leaving the Pole sputtering and fuming. He brandished his cane a few times, threatened to call the police, and with a few filthy oaths took leave of us.

Our friends were still nervous, still squirming in their seats. They began wondering aloud if he would indeed fetch a gendarme. Again we assured them that they were within their rights, that there was nothing to worry about.

"If they chase you out", I said, "they will have to chase us out too. They can't do that to us, we're Americans."

"That's just it", said one of them. "You have rights, we have none. An American! What I would give to have your passport!"

Though they only half understood what I said I went on talking to them. I couldn't bear to see them trembling. I thought of all sorts of crazy things to regale them — what a great champion Benny Leonard was, for instance, and how such and such a Jew was a Mayor, another a Governor, another a Justice of the Supreme Court ... and who knows, one day we might have a Jewish president of the United States. (After which the deluge — to myself.) I spoke of Otto Kahn, the banker and patron of the arts, of Jacob Wassermann, the novelist, even of Al Jolson. Finally I said that I was half-Jewish myself. Mona looked at me reprovingly, fearful, I suppose, that I would reveal her ancestry. And all the while I was trying to think of the title of that story by Jean Malaquais ... was it "Marianka"? The story of a pogrom which I have never been able to get, out of my mind. It leapt to my mind now with a fresh reality.

Gradually they emerged from their traumas. They even began to joke a little, tell us anecdotes about their villages. Finally one of them began to sing, but softly, smothering his voice as fearful that the Pole might return and crack him over the head. As I listened I thought of my days as a clerk in the cement company and how each week I would buy another record of Sirota's, which meant that I had to go without lunch the whole week or at best buy myself a Hershey's chocolate almond bar. I saw myself sitting in the parlor in that gloomy house in the Street of Early Sorrows, listening alone to my beloved cantor, the cantor of cantors, the king of kings. I would listen over and over to the same record, the tears streaming down my face. And my mother saying — "What on earth do you see in such music? It sounds awful to me." The more "awful" it sounded — I knew what she meant by awful — the more I liked it. He couldn't get awful enough for me. I had become one of them, a lamb waiting to be sacrificed to the unmentionable One. *Adonai! Adonai!* Sometimes, the tears still wet on my cheeks, I would dash out of the house, as if on fire, and roam the streets in ecstasy. I talked with Solomon and David, with Esther and Ruth; I walked the green pastures with Jonathan and David. To quiet down I might stop in at the stationery store run by the good Mister Cohen from Calgary and talk to him about simple things, never letting on for a moment that I was all jazzed up about Sirota. And he would hand me a five cent cigar on leaving, thank me for calling on him, and was there anything he could do for us, just mention it. Sometimes I wanted to say: "Yes, convert my old lady to Judaism!"

One by one they left us, our frightened little doves. Soon we had the compartment all to our selves. We were nearing the border, I imagined.

"God, Val", said Mona after a long silence", You should have been a Jew".

"I *am* one, in a way", I replied.

A pause.

"I wonder what Sid Essen would have done had he heard that stupid Pole shout at us? He wouldn't have taken it lying down, I'm certain of that."

No response.

I closed my eyes and started snoozing. All of a sudden the door was shoved back and some one gave me a nudge. I looked up and there were the Romanian immigration officials. "Passports, please!" We handed them our passports and they went off, apparently to examine

them at leisure somewhere. It seemed ages
before they returned. They mo-
tioned us to collect our baggage
and follow them.

"What's up?" I said.

"It's probably my pass-
port", said Mona.

In the station they began
questioning Mona with the
aid of an interpreter. As best
I could follow it, the trouble
had to do with her grandparents.
Probably they had slipped out of
the country illegally. The whole business
seemed absurd and nonsensical to me.

Finally I heard her tell them that she had an uncle in Czernowitz who
could probably explain things better than she could. Might she
telephone him?

I could see, when she gave them his name, that it registered favorably.
They now offered us some cold drinks and cigarettes.

It took some time to get through to her uncle. The train meanwhile
had left. Finally the call came through and after an excited five minutes
of conversation, Mona handed the receiver to the official who held
her passport. When he hung up we were informed that her uncle
would arrive in three quarters of an hour or so. We were free to take
a stroll, if we wished. He spoke as if everything had been satisfactorily
arranged. All he was concerned about now, it seemed to me, was how
big a gratuity he would receive for his services.

Finally the uncle arrived — in a troika. He was a big, stout man, very much the business man, thoroughly sure of himself and quite at ease in disposing of our pesky officials. He seemed genuinely delighted to see us, proud, indeed, to be able to exhibit *his* beautiful niece.

As we drove along I had the feeling of being already in Russia. "Horses! What horses!" And those jingling bells. The churches looked Byzantine, modest little gems set in drab, squalid villages. Russia, Russia. We were getting nearer and nearer to it. How wonderful it would be to set foot on that soil made sacred by Dostoievsky, Tolstoy, Pushkin, Gorky, Turgeniev, Andreyev, Lermontov and all the mad dreamers who had written of the brotherhood of man! And where was Bukovina, where that tiny village in which Mona had seen the light of day? What a glorious thing to visit the land of one's birth! If I could only see the house in which she was born it seemed to me it would wipe out all the lies she had ever told me. It didn't matter now whether her father had once owned a string of racehorses or flown kites from the roof of their home in Vienna. It was the Carpathian background I had to verify. And the Gypsy blood.

The horses were trotting gaily onward, farting now and then in their frisky way. I sank deeper into my seat, puffing away at the fat cigar her uncle had handed me. What a life! And I was just a Brooklyn boy, as Ulric used to say. Who knows, maybe one day I'd be riding into Moscow or Petersburg looking for the lost brotherhood of man.

I can't recall any longer what the house looked like from the outside, only that it was a big sprawling affair, probably an old farm house. It must have been in the suburbs of Czernowitz and quite isolated. I seem to remember the smell of pigs, of chicken manure, the sound of geese cackling and the neighing of horses. Most of all I remember the flies. We had won out over the bedbugs only to battle anew with flies and cockroaches. What could one expect? We were now in the heart of the Balkans, right at the frontier of dear old Russia, and who in his senses would complain of flies and cockroaches, dirt and disorder, or idleness and laziness, or lice and dandruff?

I've forgotten all the rooms except the huge dining room which swarmed with flies night and day, but particularly at mealtime. One of the sons, who looked like a street Arab, always circulated about the table with a huge fan brushing the flies from our food. Now and then, with the moist towel which was slung over his shoulder, he would swat a lazy one, and with a deft movement of the wrist sweep it on to the floor. Sometimes he stamped on it, in his bare feet, to make sure it would not bother us again. When he did this his eyes gleamed like a madman's. Often, despite his valiant efforts, a fly would get into one's mouth along with a hunk of food.

The mother never sat down to table with us. Her duty was to keep running back and forth to the kitchen, collecting the dirty plates and setting clean ones before us for the next course. The old man, as may be surmised, was a glutton; he could put it away like a stevedore. Naturally he was perpetually perspiring; sometimes the sweat rolled into his mouth and he would lick it with a wry grin. He was constantly complaining too, ordered his hag of a wife around like a slave, even swore at her now and then. She had grown used to it evidently, because she never talked back, never corrected him. Her face was a study in grief and woe; never once did I see her smile. Her garments were filthy and ragged and one suspected that she slept in them. To add to the picture of woe which she habitually presented she wore a wig, parted in the middle, the color of which reminded one of bedbugs. The flies didn't bother her at all; they roamed all over her at will, even into her eyes and nostrils. Now and then she sneezed, as if to shoo them away.

I never knew exactly who the members of the family were who ate with us. Sometimes we were five or six, sometimes ten or eleven. None of them bore any resemblance to the other members of the family. They looked as if they might have been collected from the street at random. As for conversation there was none, except between the uncle and us. Occasionally one of them would burst into an hysterical giggle, which no one paid any attention to. Sometimes a loud fart went off, followed by a stench fit to kill a horse. One of the older boys, who looked like a horse thief and wore fancy clothes, would sometimes take a pair of dice from his pocket and roll them on the table. After which he would make the sign of the cross. His eyes were constantly riveted on Mona; even when she went to the bathroom, I felt that his eyes were following her. He was already on the way to becoming a filthy *Goniff.*

The food was neither good nor bad. It was plentiful, that was the most one could say about it. Frequently I hadn't the slightest idea what I was eating. We ate until we belched. Toward the end the wooden toothpicks were passed around. The Uncle kept his own in his vest pocket; it was a silver one with a pearl handle. He used it very dextrously, and always from behind his napkin. He was a man of the world.

The town itself has faded from memory. We didn't get to town very often. Certainly, from all I had heard of Bucharest, Czernowitz couldn't hold a candle to it. How the days passed remains a mystery to me. Outdoors we played all sorts of simple games and in the evening checkers, dominoes or cards. We drank lots of beer and wine with seltzer water in it. It was a thoroughly uninteresting and unhealthy life we led, and I would wonder sometimes what we were doing here in this God-awful hole.

I would wonder, and remember ... just how we had got here ...

It was over a year ago and I had strolled over to Central Park and flung myself on the grass ... My money was gone, there was nothing more to do. *The dance mania* – I was still thinking on it. Still climbing that

steep flight of steps to the place
I first met Mona, the hairy
Greek in the ticket booth
putting out his paw to
grab the money ("Yes,
she'll be here soon",
though often she didn't
show up at all.) In the
corner the colored
musicians working
like fury, sweating,
panting, wheezing,
grinding it out hour
after hour with
scarcely a let-up. No
fun in it for them, nor
for the girls either, tell the
truth. One had to be screwy to
patronize such a dive. A purgatorial hole through and through: a hole
in the flap pocket of a demon whose punishment it was to masturbate
himself to death.

Other scenes came to mind. At home, for instance, with O'Mara or
Ulric looking while we danced good-naturedly, she in her Chinese
shift, me in my pyjamas. Suddenly not dancing ... just standing there
(on an imaginary man-hole), the phonograph still going, then lifting
the latch and inserting the key. Dancing again, if you could call it that.
Moving together like Siamese twins on stilts. What agony, what bliss.

("You don't do that to a friend", I can hear O'Mara saying. However,
he was always patient. One day it would be his turn — when I'd be out
for a stroll, say. Nor could I hold it against him.)

I never really knew a real dancer with whom it was a pleasure to dance. They were always preserving themselves for public exhibitions. Sex didn't enter into it with them. They didn't seem to care about dancing, only to exhibit their art. Their faces told the story. Too sharply drawn, too earnestly earnest. Muscle, not cunt.

In the midst of these reflections I remember the Park again, two girls sitting on a knoll just above me. One has her legs bent like a jack-knife, she's fully exposed. Reclining on an elbow, I pretend to be studying a blade of grass. I keep staring and staring, discreetly, to be sure. Gradually, almost imperceptibly, her legs open more and more; I can see, or imagine I can, a pinkish sliver of meat. Now its quivering, just a trifle. I raise my eyes; she's looking straight into mine. She holds it a moment, then drops her eyes and gathers a handful of grass. Returning to her original posture, she slides her bottom toward me, ever so little. I can see more distinctly now – it's like a snail coming out of its shell. Or is it my imagination?

All the while she's carrying on a conversation with her friend, who suspects nothing. At least, it would seem so. On the other hand, who knows? Maybe she's saying to her friend: "Let's see if he notices *this* …" as she gives her twat a spasmic jerk. The hell of it is twilight's coming on. The ground is still warm and the fragrance of the grass even stronger now. Fortunately no one has yet intruded upon the scene.

By now I've got an erection fit to kill. Cautiously I slide my free hand down my leg and unbutton my fly. Just one button. I glance up to see if she's observed this manoeuvre. She has indeed. Moving her position a little, she drops a hand in front of her, as if to hide her crack. The next instant she moves her hand aside, as if to say – "Can you see it better now?" I reply by opening another button. I don't dare let my prick out – it's the clink for that, in Central Park – but I know it's well in view. With my hand cupped over it, and reclining on my side as I am, only she can see what's happening. Now she stretches her legs out, leaving one of them crooked. She's begun to move rhythmically, gently, as one moves to sleep. Her friend meanwhile has turned face down on the grass.

Leisurely now I remove my hat and place it strategically. Time to let horsey out of the stable. How he jerks about! Like a hungry nag trying to extract the last bit of oats from his feed bag. The girl is moving more excitedly. Bolder and bolder. Her mouth is twitching, her face crimson. Is it my imagination again or is it really a trickle I see oozing from between her legs? I fasten my gaze intently. Don't dare move an inch closer. Yes, something *is* dribbling from that crack. It looks like white mucilage. At this point I simply can't hold it any longer. Whee-eee-eee! Out it spurts, the seed of Onan. With this the mare above gives a few short, quick jerks and flops over on her side. ("What a day!") She lies like that a few moments, then pulls herself up a bit and opens her legs as wide as possible. I can see the goo all over her hair and trickling down her legs.

What now? I fling myself face forward on the grass and wait. Not a stir from any of us. It's almost dark now.

Now they're stirring. They're getting to their feet. I quickly button my fly and sit up. She's coming to greet me.

(For one moment I had a feeling that it was a painting coming to life, one of those fleshy, lascivious *al fresco* things out of the Renaissance. Eve holding an apple in her hand while a snake winds slowly toward her belly button.)

"Excuse me", she says, extracting a cigarette from a silver case, "but can you give me a light?"

(Was it my condition or the way she said it? I could swear she was speaking Italian.)

I couldn't move my lips, I was that unstrung. I fished out the matches and held a light to her cigarette.

She came closer. "Did you like it?" she says, looking me straight in the eye.

I moved my head slightly and gave a grunt of pleasure.

"What do we do now?" she says.

I'm still tongue-tied.

"There must be other places ..."

"*Where?*" I stammer.

She ignored this and turned to beckon her friend.

Recovering my voice, I hastily explained that it was impossible to go anywhere, that I was flat broke. "I've already been everywhere", I said, and it sounded terribly lame.

"I'd like to see more of *that*", she said, tapping it with the back of her hand.

As her girl friend joined us she added: "She feels left out. Amy's her name. Mine's Suzanne."

"Let's sit down a moment", said I. "Let's talk it over."

"You're trembling", said Amy.

We sat down, the girls on either side of me. As we did so we burst out laughing, all three of us.

"In Central Park!" exclaimed Suzanne.

"Lie on your side again, won't you", said Amy. "I'd like to feel it, once, before we go."

I did as commanded. She put her hand over it and immediately it began to rise.

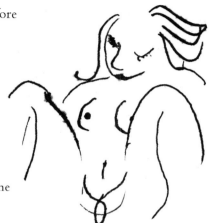

"Let's get out of here!" said Suzanne.

"Yes, let's!" said Amy. "Let's go home ... You'll come, won't you."

I started to explain once again that I was broke. Where did they live? Was it far?

To all this Suzanne said *Phut!* She'd call a cab, it was only a few blocks distant, there was nothing to be embarrassed about, and so on.

Amy laughed. A beautiful pearly laugh she had. Suddenly I was aware how good looking she was.

As if to put me more at ease Suzanne remarked that they were never jealous of one another.

"Yes", said Amy, "we don't mind sharing you."

I couldn't help wondering, seeing how eager they were, if there would be enough to share.

It was only a hop, skip and jump to their flat which was on the second floor of an old fashioned brownstone house. Beyond the fact that they were going to fix a good meal soon as we arrived, nothing much was said up to this point. They didn't ask where I hailed from, what I did for a living, or anything of that sort.

135

Yes, they were extraordinarily amiable, the two of them. Definitely not sluts either. What had happened in the park was a lark. Could happen to anyone, aside from invalids and crotchets (And why not? I asked myself. A warm day, nobody around … even decent girls get that way sometimes. What more natural than to spread your legs and let someone have a look? Worse things than that happened to some of the venerable characters in the Bible.)

"Maybe you'd like to take a shower first", said Suzanne, as we entered.

"What about a drink?" said Amy.

"A shower first, then a drink", said I.

What luck! I thought to myself, as I stood under the shower. Such good-hearted, good-natured, clean, healthy girls! "All this and heaven too!"

As I was drying off Amy stuck her head in. Couldn't resist having a peep at it. "We'll have *you* later, Mister" she said, pecking at it with her soft, warm lips. "How do you like your chops — well done?"

"Righto!"

Meanwhile Suzanne had undressed. She was waiting for me to step out. The hair on her cunt was dewy and bristly. I ran my hand up her crotch to make sure it wasn't all a dream.

"You'll give me a good fuck, won't you darling?" she said.

"I hope so", I said. "Open it a little, will you?"

She parted her lips. Almost like a priest breaking bread.

"Don't let Amy drain you", she said, holding her cunt open for me to inspect.

Amy knocked at the door. Dinner would soon be ready. "No cheat-ing!"

I made for the door. "Tell me one thing", I said. "Do you often come like that without being touched?"

"Darling", she answered, "when I saw it pop out at me I almost fainted. I don't care what you do to me. Fuck me like a dog, if you want. I've never been so excited."

"Come here", I said. "Take it in your mouth a moment."

Her lips twitched again, as they had in the Park. She closed her mouth over it, gobbled a few times, then pulled away. "No, save it, save it!" she begged. "I want it every way you can do it . . . *later.*"

I found Amy standing at the stove. I put my arms around her and kissed her playfully. She slid her tongue down my throat. Then she pushed me away, kittenish like.

"Let me get on with this", she said. "We have lots of time."

"Oh", she called, as I stepped into the living room, "I forgot to fix you a drink. What would you like?"

"Anything", I said. "I'm not fussy."

"Good", she said, standing in the doorway. "Then you're not a drinker. That's just dandy. Then you'll have a mind for the important thing. I love to be fucked, but not by a drunk." She raised her skirt and placed my hand on her cunt. "Christ!" she groaned, fishing out my prick, "Christ!" she groaned, "Keep it that way, will you?" And let *me* have it first, *please!*" She bent down and put it in her mouth. Only for a moment. "God, it's good", she said. "Men get what they want when they want it, don't they?"

137

I told her she was adorable. I promised her a royal fuck. "And after that", I added, "we'll get acquainted. It's good this way, not knowing anything about the other. All I know is you're a hot little bitch; just to look at you makes me horny. Listen, what about the chops? Don't let them burn!"

She hustled back to the kitchen and I nestled down in an easy-chair and sipped the drink Amy had fixed me. I couldn't make out what it was but it tasted delicious.

From the kitchen Amy shouted: "Just wait, *you*. We'll make you do it till you're weak in the knees."

More and more the whole thing seemed like a dream. A delicious wet dream. I could well imagine what lay in store for me. But why *me*? What had I done to deserve this?

For an instant Mona flitted through my mind. If she could see me now! And she, what was *she* doing at this moment? Further speculation on that score was interrupted by Suzanne's entrance. She had rigged herself up in a fetching negligee. As she fixed herself a drink she looked at me, as if approvingly and said: "You're married, aren't you?"

I nodded. And smiled.

"I thought so", she said. "That's good. *You know why?*"

It was the first direct inquiry either of them had made and the motive was a happy one.

It was a good meal Amy had prepared and we had some excellent Chianti to go with it. During the course of conversation I discovered that Suzanne had been on the stage. Amy was a model. What they were doing presently they didn't say and I didn't ask. The talk flowed easily: they were most frank and candid about their intimate experiences.

Almost shamelessly so, I thought. But, as Amy remarked, it was the occasion of a lifetime. Since we had begun as we did there was no reason to suddenly become discreet or inhibited. It was fun to tell a perfect stranger all that was on your mind. Especially to one who promised you a good fuck.

Physically an utter contrast, they were mentally and emotionally much alike. Almost like sisters. Suzanne, the taller one, was the type the French call "*une fausoe naigre*". She had dark hair and deep blue eyes. Her legs were exquisitely tanned. Her dark hair, thick under the armpits (which I liked), contrasted with her pale olive skin; the mouth was rather large but beautifully curved. A thin layer of down covered her upper lip. Amy, on the other hand, was blonde, blonde as blonde could be, with a body that was lush and vibrant. She had unusually large brown eyes with long silken lashes. Her teats were full and firm with nipples like tiny strawberries. All through the meal she sat with her boobies exposed; now and then, when she became excited, she caressed them. But it was the shape of her head that fascinated me. It belonged to one of Renoir's women — round, foreshortened, the mouth very sensual and a natural bright red. She was the seductive cub, Amy. Suzanne had the poise of the actress. Both were free and unrestrained, yet never vulgar — at least to my way of thinking — even when their actions verged on the obscene. Indeed, it was this which made them so alluring and bewitching — this ability to be sensual and provocative without being coarse and vulgar.

It was during the meal, for example, that Suzanne rose suddenly and, opening her negligee, rubbed the palm of her hand suggestively down her abdomen. She was illustrating how a certain striptease artist went about it. As her hand slid over the Mons Venus, she said: "If only they would do *this* some time!" And so saying, she gently parted the lips of her vagina. "Wouldn't that be fetching?" she said, and sat down.

We refilled the glasses and we drank to one another. Amy, I noticed, was unusually excited. Cupping her breasts she fixed me with a hungry look and said: "Do us a favour, will you? Take it out and let's see how big it is!" Losing no time, she rose and came to my side. "Let *me* unbutton it!" she murmured. I stood up and, while Amy fished around — she had to squeeze my balls first — I fastened my gaze on Suzanne. What a picture she presented — leaning on her elbows, her head thrust forward as if to bite it off, her lips parted, heavily moist. As Amy pulled it out — I had a sort of sluggish hard on — Suzanne's lips began to tremble and twitch, like they had in the Park. I beckoned her to come close. "Let me feel your cunt", I said. "I'll bet you're coming again." Sure enough, she was all wet, all gooey. Amy now had my prick half-way down her throat. Her whole body was quivering. Giving a little groan, she drew her mouth away, placed one foot on the chair beside her, then grabbed my cock and put it between her legs. "I can't wait", she gasped. "Do it now, *quick!*" I slid it in part way, raised her off the ground to let her clasp her legs around me, and rammed it home. Suzanne watching, her face spread wide, eyes popping with lust and envy. It was a short, quick fuck, but Amy was happy. As I pulled away she gasped and came again. "Sometimes she can't stop coming", said Suzanne, choking on the words.

Amy went to the
kitchen to prepare
the coffee. Suzanne
and I resumed our
places at the table.

"Now I'd like a real
drink", I said. "Have you
any brandy ... or Kummel?"

"We've got some *delicious*
cognac", said Suzanne, throwing her arms
around me and kissing me hungrily. "Anything to keep that thing
alive, my dear. God, how long must I wait? You're driving me crazy,
do you know it?"

Amy reappeared with a strawberry shortcake smothered in whipped
cream. She had nothing on now but a scarlet blouse open at the top.
Her teats stood out tauntingly. I took a good look at her cunt; the hair
was just as blonde as her cute little poll. And thick and curly. She
looked utterly ravishing. "Now I can wait", she said. "I've had a taste."

"If I had to go insane", said Suzanne, "I'd want it to be watching you
two fuck". Then she added: "Sometimes I wish I were a man. It must
be wonderful to get an erection, especially a slow, lingering one. Like
a horse grazing contentedly and suddenly, for no reason, out it comes
and dangles before your eyes. It must be fun to masturbate – with a
thing like that in your hand. Something to handle, what! Jesus, there's
no getting away from it, a prick *is* something ... something you can't
ignore. Give me a drink, someone ... I'm all a-tremble. It was bad
enough in the Park, but to sit here and watch the two of you go at it
... whew! It's too much. I'd like to cut it off and just keep it for
myself ..."

Your turn's coming", said Amy sweetly. She disappeared into the kitchen to fetch the coffee. I had to look twice at those buttocks of hers, they were so absolutely perfect.

Once again we relaxed, over the coffee. The shortcake was heavenly.

"It's too bad", I remarked, as I spooned up some of the heavily whipped cream, "it's too bad we're not a foursome".

Her face flushed, her eyes flashing, Suzanne exclaimed – "You're wrong there, it's perfect the way it is. If we *were* four, I'd want the extra one to be a girl not a man. You're the cock in the barnyard. We're just hens. We wait our turn, and we like it that way. I mean it! Only hens don't get the fun out of watching what we do, do they? Just to see you ease it out is something. One good prick – like yours – is all we need. Right, Amy?"

Amy smiled indulgently. "Suzanne is truly lecherous", she said, licking her words. "I don't think any man can satisfy her. When she's really hot, why ... well, I've seen her take a ..." She turned and pointed to a long, thin black candle standing on the chest of drawers.

"Oh come!" said Suzanne. "That happened just once."

"But the way you went at it!" Amy's big eyes opened wide.

"How do you mean?" said I.

"Well ...", said Amy.

"Let me tell it myself", said Suzanne. She turned to me and, looking into my eyes with a tantalizing expression, she said: "Do you really want to hear it?"

"I sure do." I turned and took another look at the candle. "Did you get it in all the way?" I asked.

Amy began to giggle. "Show him!" she said. "I dare you!"

"I'll do nothing of the kind", said Suzanne. "Not tonight, at least. Tonight I'm going to have *that!*" She pointed to my fly.

"Tell us about it then", I urged. "You're not ashamed to do that, are you?"

It wasn't shame that held her back, she just didn't know where to begin. So it seemed, at any rate.

She leaned forward and put her hand on my arm, as if to make sure I would understand. Then she smiled, one of those dreamy, retrospective smiles which can be so meaningful.

143

"Pour me some brandy, please", she said. She took a quick gulp, then addressing me, she said: "Have you ever seen a pornographic film?"

I shook my head. "Never had the chance", I replied.

"Then you have no idea what it's like. It's more than you can imagine, believe me. Anyway, I saw one ... my first and only one ... at a friend's home one night. I'll do my best to describe it, but it's all so confusing. There's no story, you see, no acting. (You can't *pretend* to fuck, can you?) It opened ...", she burst out laughing. "It opened with a close up of a woman's crotch. Her face was hidden. All you could see was her huge buttocks and a rather large, ugly-looking gash. She was playing with herself, lazy-like, dreamy-like, as if she were half asleep. Then the pelvis began to move, to rotate, slowly at first, then more and more animatedly. The lips of her vagina were very large, like those African women you hear tell about ..."

She paused to take another sip of brandy.

"The opening was startling enough ... almost terrifying, to tell you the truth. But the next shot was even more so, and thoroughly unexpected. As I told you, there's no sequence to these things, unless it's getting down to business as quickly as possible. Well, the next thing was a man fully dressed with a cap on. A thin, scroungy-looking type, like a gutter rat. He starts right in taking off his trousers. Immediately his prick begins to rise, slowly, steadily ... an enormous tool, honest, bigger than anything I ever hope to see again. There he stood, shaking it at us and making the filthiest grimaces as he did so. An absolute degenerate. You know, the kind you're always afraid you'll encounter in some dark alley. It was disgusting, yet frightfully exciting. I felt that I was seeing something I ought never to see — or that I might never see again."

She paused again, searching for the proper words to express what followed.

"From the other corner of the screen comes a woman now, stark naked and homely as sin, but with a voluptuous body. She goes down on him. It takes ages for him to come. Meanwhile you see her mouth working as she licks it, gobbles it, sucks it in and out, swallows it alive. (Believe me you can learn something from these degenerates!) Anyway, finally he draws it out, inch by inch . . . it's ever so long, incredible really, and it's curving the other way now. When he gets it out completely he calmly squirts a load right in her mouth. That too was unbelievable — the way he continued to squirt. Just like a bull! The scene changes and now they're in bed, him with his cap on still. She's on hands and knees, and he's giving it to her dog fashion. What a pair of balls! You see them swinging like brass knockers. He goes at it like an animal — not that there's anything wrong with *that*! And the harder he fucks, the more she wiggles her ass. Sometimes it looked as if her eyes would roll out of her head. Naturally I had an orgasm, two or three perhaps. I thought he'd never stop. A perpetual hard on, if ever there was one. Sometimes he'd pull out all the way and she'd have to reach under, grab it, slip it in for him. She looked delirious each time that happened. Who wouldn't? And by the way, when he pulled out like that you could see how slimy his prick was, as if he'd rubbed it with vaseline or dipped it in olive oil. (Let's remember the olive oil, Amy. I want to see what it feels like when it's oiled.) Every now and then he'd jab her extra hard and then she'd groan . . . such a groan . . . such deep pleasure in it! When he's through with her another girl appears — a slinky lascivious bitch with kinky hair and eyes like a deer's. She has to suck him off first. And how! An artist at it, using her fingers, twining them round his balls and all that, while making her lips and mouth perform the most astonishing feats. It was maddening, I tell you, especially when the camera moved in close and all you could see were those huge balls of his swinging like bells and that slimy piston plunging in and out of her cunt. Any woman would die to be fucked like that. Like an animal I mean ..."

She stopped. "Go on", we urged. "Don't stop now."

"Well, that was that ... as much as I remember now. When I got home Amy was still up. I told her about it, at length. And as I rehearsed each scene in detail I got so worked up, I was so on edge, that if I had known where to reach that degenerate bugger I would have called him up and paid him handsomely to come and fuck me. I was that bad that I was almost ready to tackle Amy — only I'm not that kind. Anyway, I undressed, had a drink or two, and the more I thought about it the more I felt I had to do something or go mad. I was sitting where you are now. Suddenly, turning my head, I caught sight of the candle over there. On the impulse I got up and grabbed it. I grabbed it like I would have if I were going for that slimy tool of his. I caressed it with two hands. It felt smooth, smooth and slippery. Inviting. "Amy", I said, "I'm going to try it. I'm going to pretend it's *him* fucking me, that beast!" And then I remembered how it looked, his long, snaky prick, when he would pull away. All gooey, icky, glistening. I got some oil and I smeared it over the candle. In doing so the tip of my finger touched the wick. Good, I thought. It'll be like a French tickler. And it was! I was so worked up, of course, that I came in no time, even though it was only partly in. I was determined to try again, get it all the way in, if I could. We worked the candle over, trying to make it more of a French tickler. We roughed it up here and there ... silly, what! But I was in the mood to fuck myself silly. This time I decided Amy was to hold the candle. I lay back, on the floor, and arched my pelvis; I rolled it around, like that slut in the film, while Amy slid it back and forth. Each time she got it in a little farther. By this time my cunt could have swallowed a rabbit. The wick, of course, drove me mad. It got way up and scratched at my womb. I kept begging her to

shove it in harder, faster. Finally it went in all the way, and then I came,
one spasm after another, like I've never come before. It was pure
agony. Maybe she didn't get it in full length, but it felt that way. No
man ever penetrated me like that, that I know. Maybe some time I'll
try a stallion. For days afterwards I could feel that candle inside me. I
was all inflamed and swollen. My mind was even more inflamed.
When I looked at a man all I could think was how big is his tool, how
thin or thick, how often he can do it, would he do it to me if I asked
him ... yes, supposing I went up to him, a degenerate, a beast, no

147

matter what, and I said: 'I'm
horny, horny, I want to be
fucked, do it will you?
Fuck me now, right here
in the street, in the elevator, anywhere …'.
Do you see what I
mean?"

She came to a full stop. Her
breasts were heaving, her face had
grown tawny, her legs were jumping, she was
twitching all over. Turning to Amy, she said: "Are you satisfied now?"

Such a lovely weekend I put in with them. A saint couldn't have asked
for more. I never stirred from their rooms till Monday morning. My
cock seemed to have grown an inch longer from all the doings; it felt
like a rubber truncheon. As I set out for work that morning I
wondered what it would be like to spend an entire week in their
company. The degenerate whom Suzanne had described so vividly
floated before my eyes. The one who kept his cap on – and his shoes
too most likely. The thought of that phallus erectus glistening like a
well-oiled piston reminded me of the olive oil. We tried it, Suzanne
and I, and it worked like a charm. Nothing like keeping one's tool
oiled. And the candle business – I understood it better after laying
Suzanne. Only once before had I slept with a woman whose cunt was
so deep yet fitted like a glove. The way she arched her pelvis, hands at
her sides, throwing it forward to catch it like a quoit, then squeezing
it with those strong clamps which most women seem not to know they
possess. And with it talking, talking to me, talking to *it*, urging,
goading, coaxing, wheedling. Her mouth expressive of every mood,
every emotion, every thought. And those blue eyes staring intently as
I withdrew. As Amy said, she was indeed a lecherous one. Cunt

through and through, mentally as well as physically. Playful at the same time, and inventive. And humorous as only a woman can be in such life and death matters.

How wonderful it would be, I thought, to have someone on the side like her to sleep with, someone with whom it would be nothing but sex. Someone, in other words, whom I could fall back on, as a relief from all the emotional conflicts. Someone who would say – "Did you bring *it* along with you?" (Like you say to a child: "You didn't forget to bring your toothbrush, did you?".) Nonchalant. You and your dingus, me and my what you may call it. With such a relationship one might be able to talk about all manner of things – earthly things and heavenly things. None of that irritating, annihilating business of – "Do you still love me?" Or – "Why don't you treat me as if I were a human being?" Et cetera.

Was it the actress in her that induced these speculations? Passionate as she was, she could also be detached. Objective, you might call it. While fucking she could observe herself fucking. It was the fucking that obsessed her. Not *her* fucking or being fucked, but fuck itself ... the wonder of it, the bottomless bottom of it,

During those thirty-six hours we did some tall-talking, the three of us. Cool, anecdotal talk mixed with tales simple and fantastic. Now and then a gem, straight from the heart. One of them, which Suzanne related of her mother, I can never forget. Briefly, it went like this ... The father, who was a judge, was much older than the mother. An austere individual, he was preoccupied with his own problems. As a consequence, the mother – probably a slut at heart – had taken to drink. When she drank she had to have a man. This sad turn in her life had occurred when Suzanne was about twelve. By the time she was sixteen her father had decided upon a divorce. He had been aware of his wife's infidelities but because of his position, and also because he was singularly devoted to his daughter, he had tried to avoid this issue. A few weeks before the parents separated Suzanne, then a senior in High School, came home one afternoon to meet with a strange sight. Her mother, stark naked, was kneeling on the floor, sucking the cock of an ugly bruiser whom she had evidently picked up in a bar. She was blind drunk, and a disgusting sight to behold, even had her lips not been closed over some utter stranger's prick.

Suzanne never saw her mother again. A few days later the poor woman committed suicide. Nor did she ever tell her father what she had witnessed.

"It took time", she said, "before I would let any man touch me. When I did give way I went the whole hog. To be fucked wasn't enough ... I wanted to *look* too. Maybe that's why I told you about that dirty film in such detail. I can never see and feel enough. It's as if I were trying to finish the job my mother began that day. I can still remember how I ran out of the room — just as she pulled her mouth away. I could still see that prick of his as it leaped out ... like a fish jumping the net."

"It may also explain", she hastened to add, "why I don't like people who drink too much ... women especially. It worries me. I fear what may happen when they lose control of themselves."

"The strange thing is", she continued, "that I never worry what may happen when it comes to sex. It was horrifying to come upon my mother like that — though she probably did the same for my father — but that isn't what bothered me ... it was the when and the where ... her utter thoughtlessness. It could have ruined my whole life. Now I say this I suddenly think of my own actions, how reckless I was, in the Park. One thinks that only perverts do such things. But I'm not a pervert ..."

Strange confession. Strange only because women
seldom talk freely and openly to men.
How they talk to one another we
know only from eavesdrop-
pers, from what our
wives and sweet-
hearts confess
when they're in a
mood to. The
talk which goes
on in the powder
room, for in-
stance, is almost a
closed book to men. All
we know, or surmise, is that
women have even filthier tongues than men. Men can be ashamed of
themselves, women hardly ever.

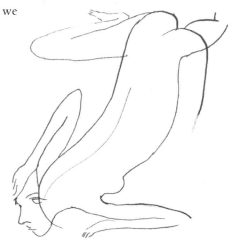

When, a few months later, I came upon Molly Bloom's soliloquy, how
tame it seemed! But then Molly Bloom was but a mouthpiece for James
Joyce. Suzanne's talk was real. It was a cunt talking, not an Irish bard.

As for Amy, let it not be thought that she was eclipsed by Suzanne. A
delightful nymphomaniac, her whole effort, it seemed to me, was
given to wearing a man down, to extract from him his last juices. With
her the thing to do was to hold back. Give her just enough to make
her come again — while counting up to a hundred. Hers was really an
inflamed cunt. Once inside her, it like ravishing a polyp. It wasn't
muscles alone which did the work but the whole fleshy pulp, as if there
were a hundred tiny, sucking, greedy maws at work. In a word, it was
an octopus she kept concealed between her legs. With her there was
no talk ... just grunts and squeals ... animal cries.

151

It was toward evening of the second day, after we had had a good snooze, and Amy begging for more, that I plucked up courage to make a suggestion. It was rather in order, all things considered.

I suggested that she have a go of it with the candle.

Suzanne clapped her hands in glee. "Yes!" she cried, "you've got to do it, Amy. Turn about's fair play."

Amy wasn't too eager to perform but, after I fished out a rather swollen, distended prick and let her nibble at it a bit, she consented. Suzanne was to be the operator. I sat back, with a drink in my hand, to enjoy it undisturbed.

Amy wasn't built like Suzanne. A banana would have suited her better than a candle. But Suzanne, determined bitch that she was, used all her art. A man would never have thought up the tricks she employed. Finally she made Amy kneel on the floor and tackled her from the rear. By now Amy was utterly delirious. Snatching the candle from Suzanne, she worked it back and forth herself. What a tableau! To see a woman being fucked by a man is something, but to see her giving herself a workout — with a candle! — is something else. That look of utter abandon which a man only half glimpses when he hurls his bolt, preoccupied as he usually is with his own feelings, that expression which I observed now, like a ringside spectator, was almost too much for me. A fury absolutely shameless gripped her. "Cut it off and leave it in there!" That was the look. The female. Insatiable female. Praying mantis.

Yes, a delicious weekend it was. Would there be more of them? I wondered. They had told me on leaving that the door was always open to me. They didn't say — "Will you be back next week?" Or, "Give me a ring in a few days!" No, they simply left the latch hanging, as it were. My pleasure was their pleasure. Blessed creatures!

I hadn't the slightest doubt that I would be visiting them frequently. What was to hinder, after all? Only one thing — sudden impotence!

How ignorant I was of the turn that events would take! How could I possibly see that in an hour or two, hardly more, these two lovely creatures, their cunts, their artifices, their delightful cameraderie, would fade out like a theorem erased from the blackboard.

And what would the catalyst be? A cablegram, no less. A cablegram lying on my desk, waiting for me to open. Signed Mona.

I could scarcely believe my eyes. There it was in black and white:

BOAT DOCKING THURSDAY. MEET ME!